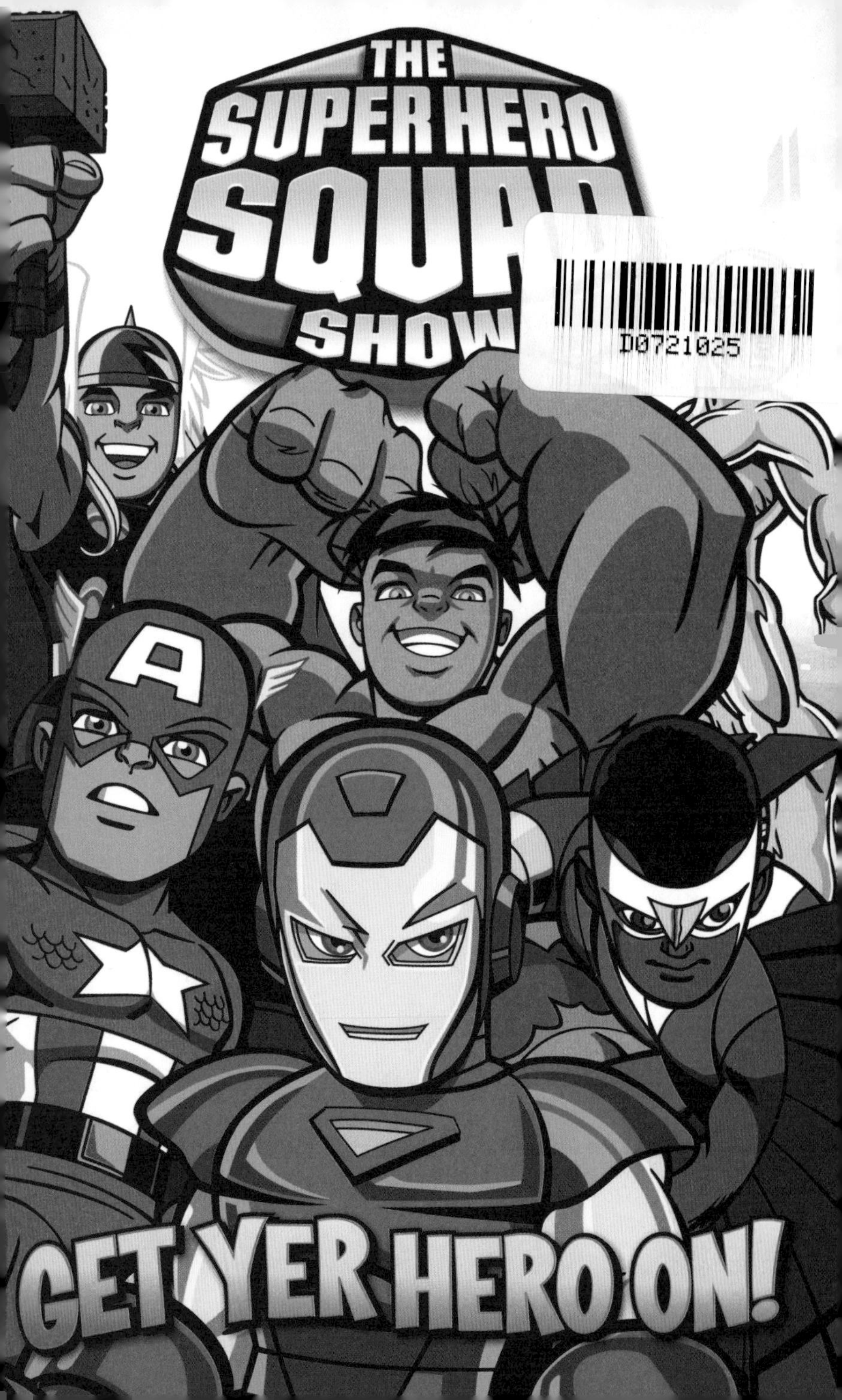
THE SUPER HERO SQUAD SHOW
GET YER HERO ON!

THE SUPER HERO SQUAD SHOW

GET YER HERO ON!

WRITER: PAUL TOBIN
ARTISTS: DARIO BRIZUELA, MARCELO DICHIARA & TODD NAUCK
COLORS: DARIO BRIZUELA & CHRIS SOTOMAYOR
LETTERERS: DAVE SHARPE & BLAMBOT'S NATE PIEKOS
VARIANT COVER ARTIST: MARCELO DICHIARA
ASSISTANT EDITOR: MICHAEL HORWITZ
EDITOR: NATHAN COSBY
SPECIAL THANKS TO COURTNEY LANE, KAT JONES,
CHRIS FONDACARO & TOM MARVELLI

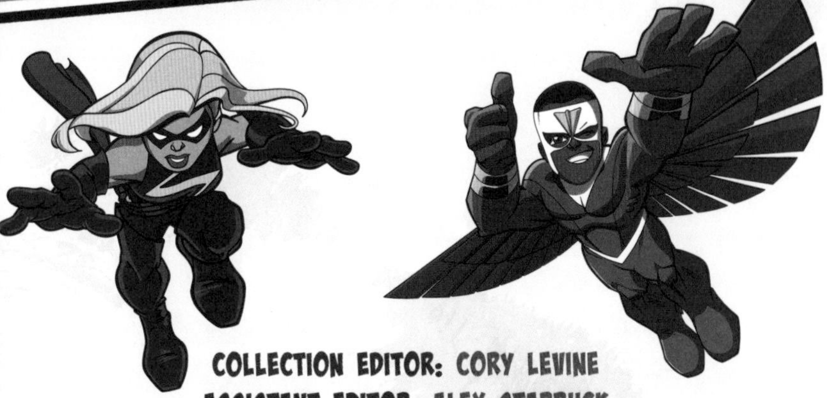

COLLECTION EDITOR: CORY LEVINE
ASSISTANT EDITOR: ALEX STARBUCK
ASSOCIATE EDITOR, SPECIAL PROJECTS: JOHN DENNING
EDITORS, SPECIAL PROJECTS: JENNIFER GRÜNWALD & MARK D. BEAZLEY
SENIOR EDITOR, SPECIAL PROJECTS: JEFF YOUNGQUIST
SENIOR VICE PRESIDENT OF SALES: DAVID GABRIEL
BOOK DESIGN: PAT MCGRATH

EDITOR IN CHIEF: JOE QUESADA
PUBLISHER: DAN BUCKLEY
EXECUTIVE PRODUCER: ALAN FINE

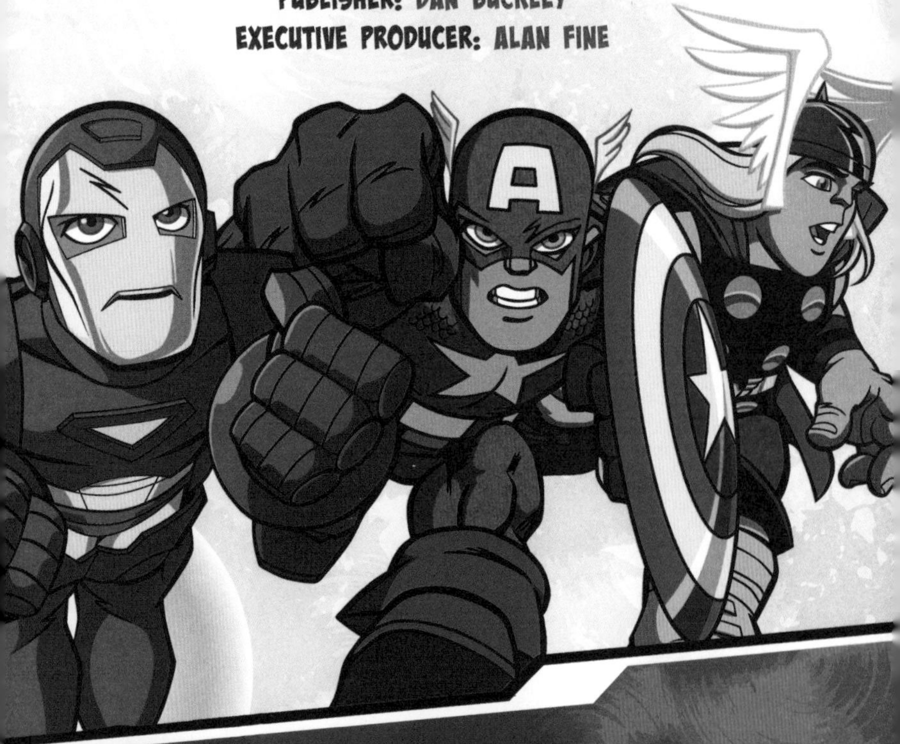

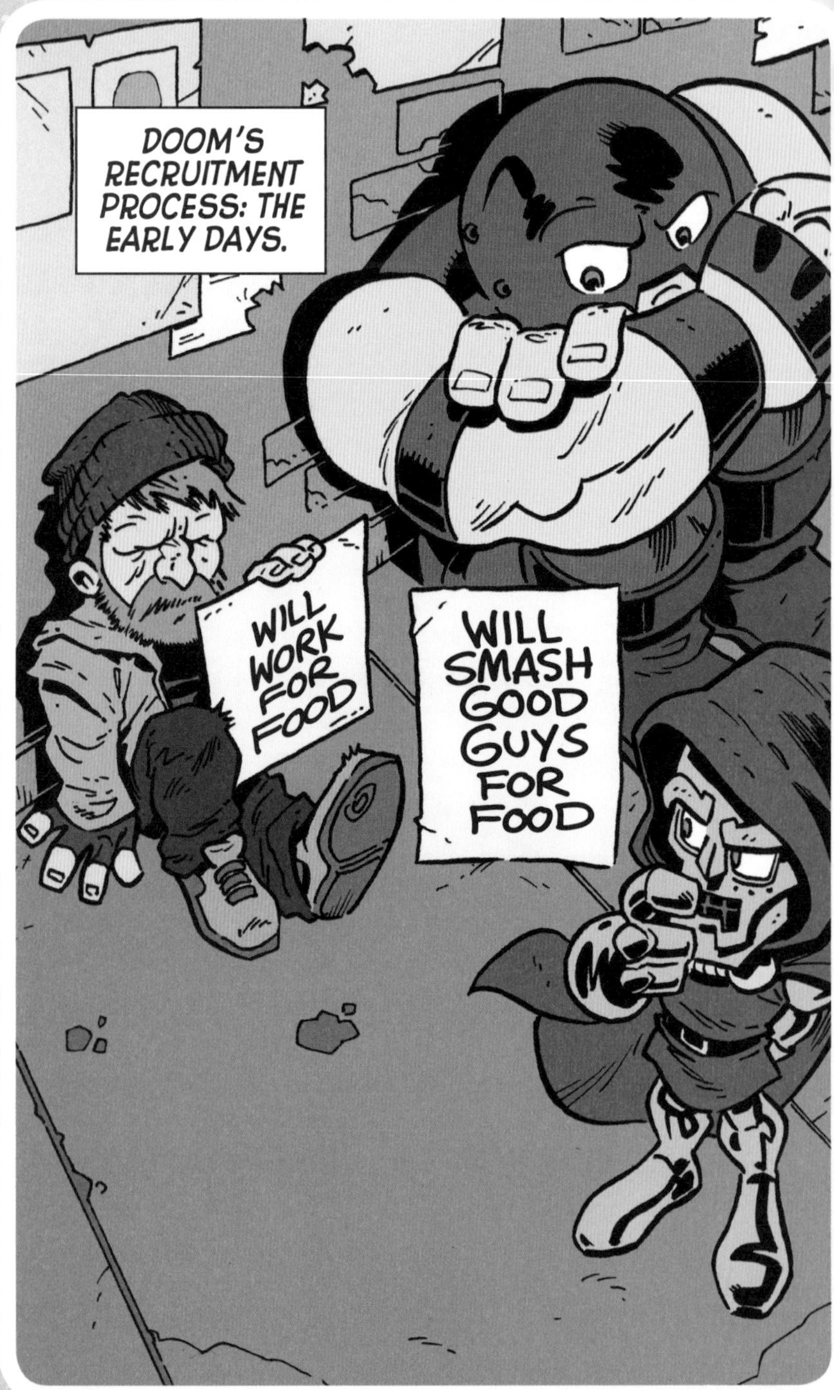
DOOM'S RECRUITMENT PROCESS: THE EARLY DAYS.
WILL WORK FOR FOOD
WILL SMASH GOOD GUYS FOR FOOD

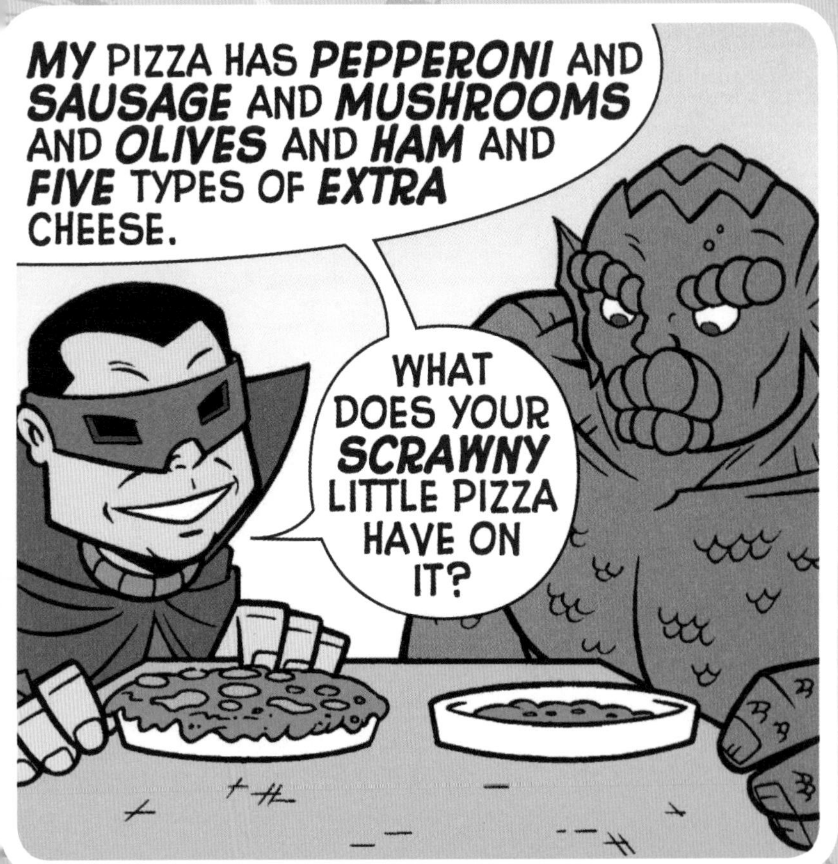
MY PIZZA HAS PEPPERONI AND SAUSAGE AND MUSHROOMS AND OLIVES AND HAM AND FIVE TYPES OF EXTRA CHEESE.
WHAT DOES YOUR SCRAWNY LITTLE PIZZA HAVE ON IT?

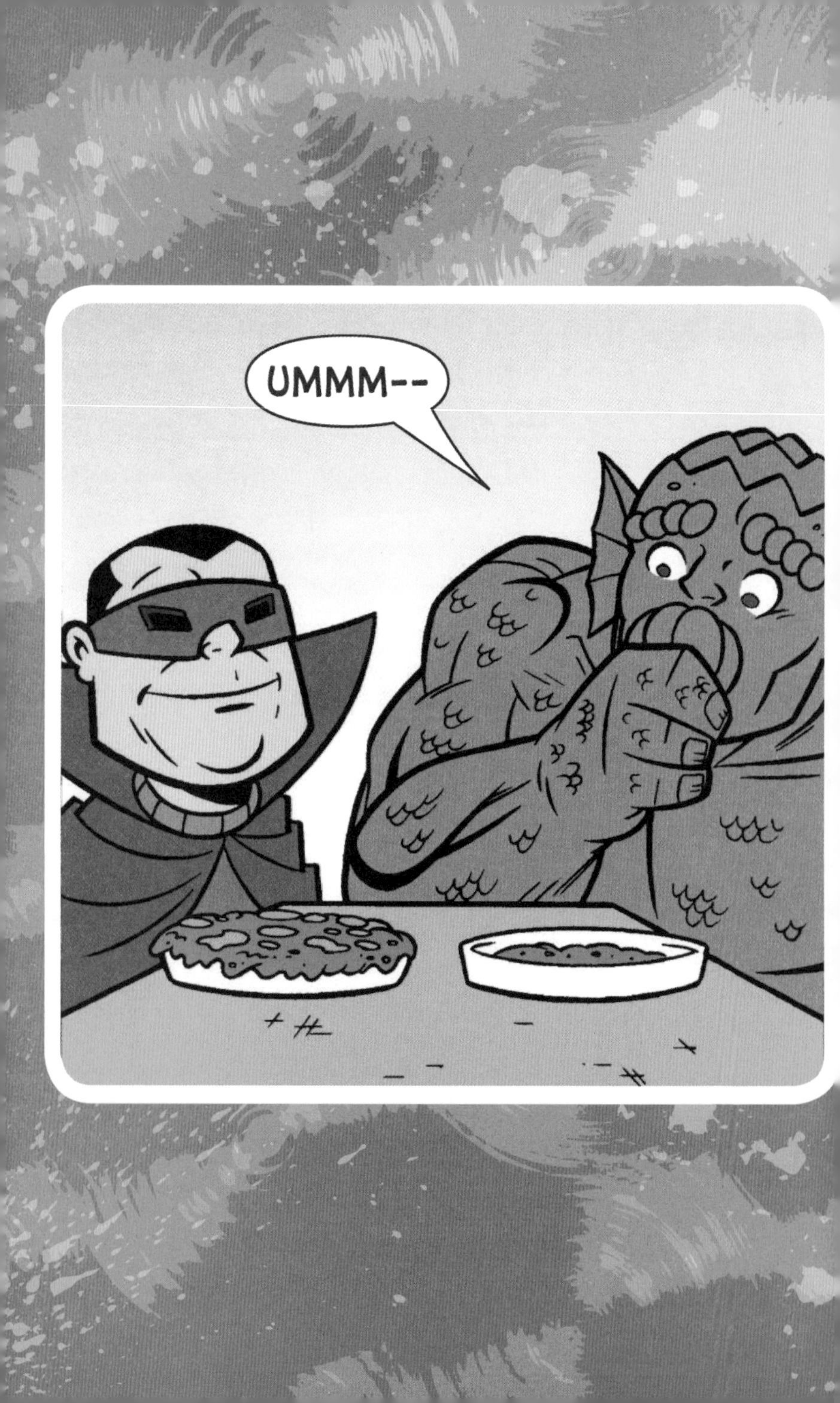
UMMM--

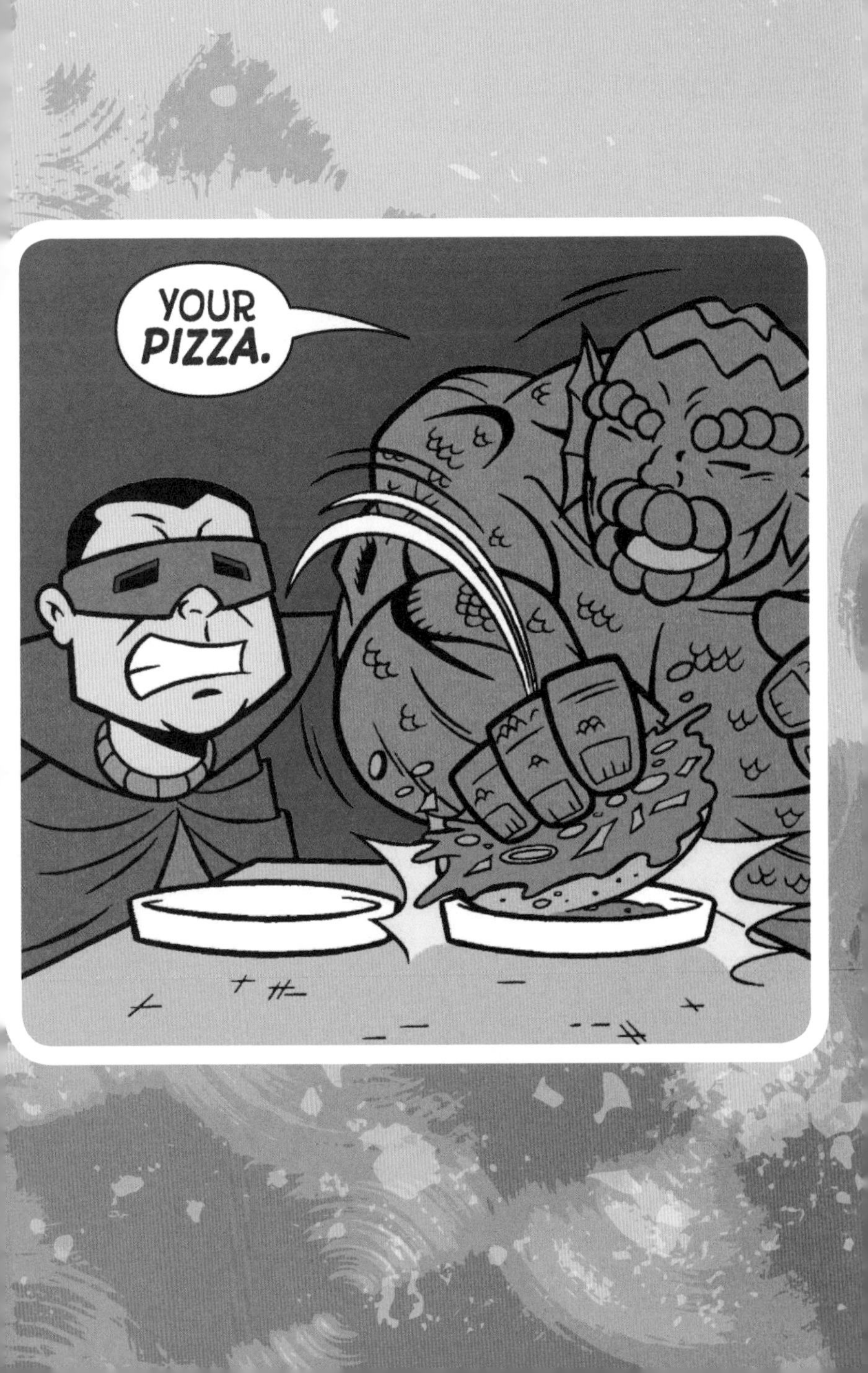
YOUR PIZZA.

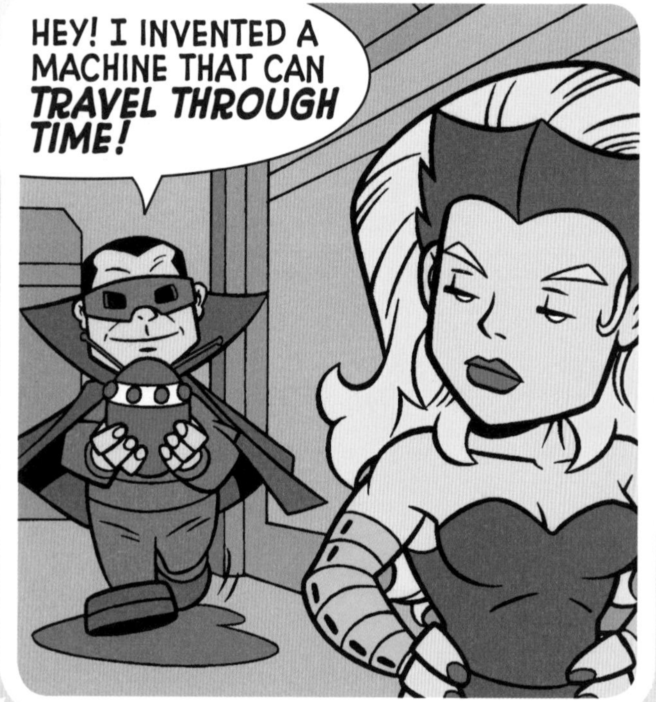
HEY! I INVENTED A MACHINE THAT CAN TRAVEL THROUGH TIME!

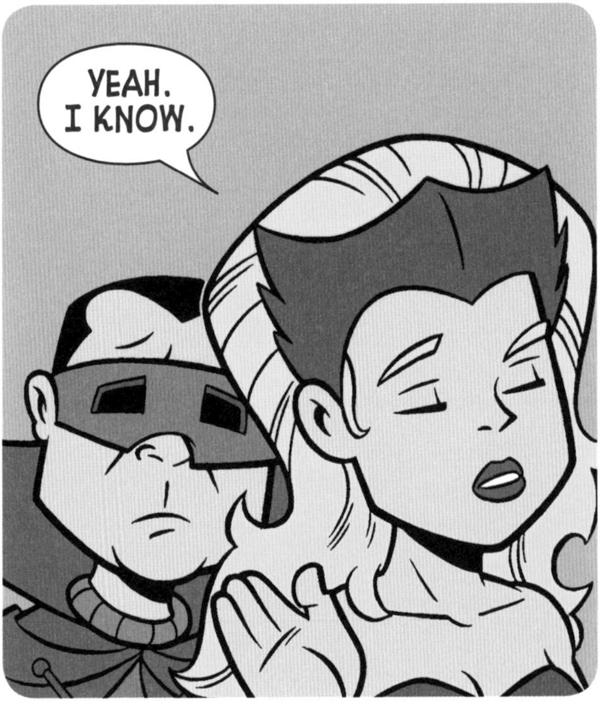
YEAH. I KNOW.

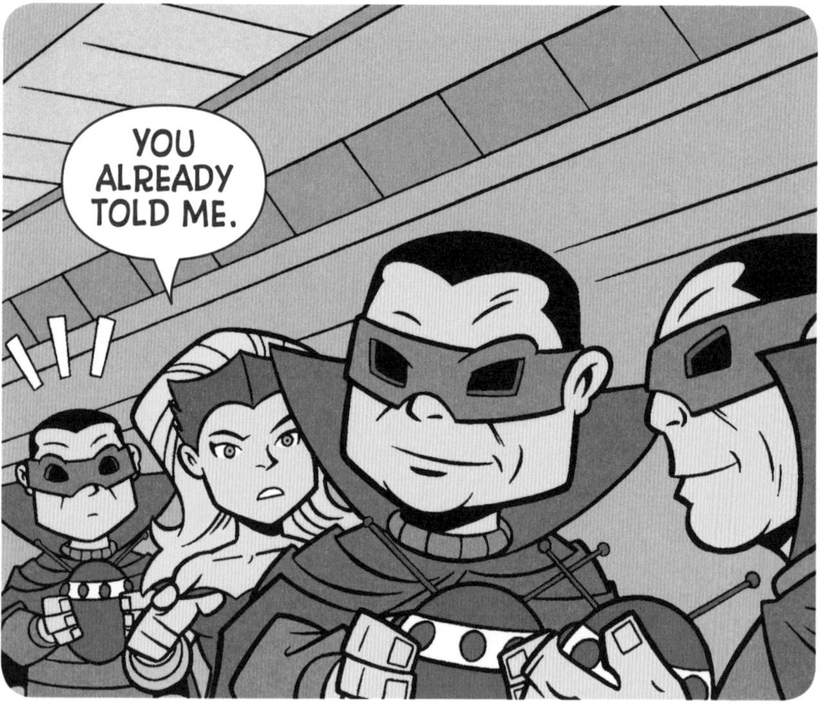
YOU ALREADY TOLD ME.

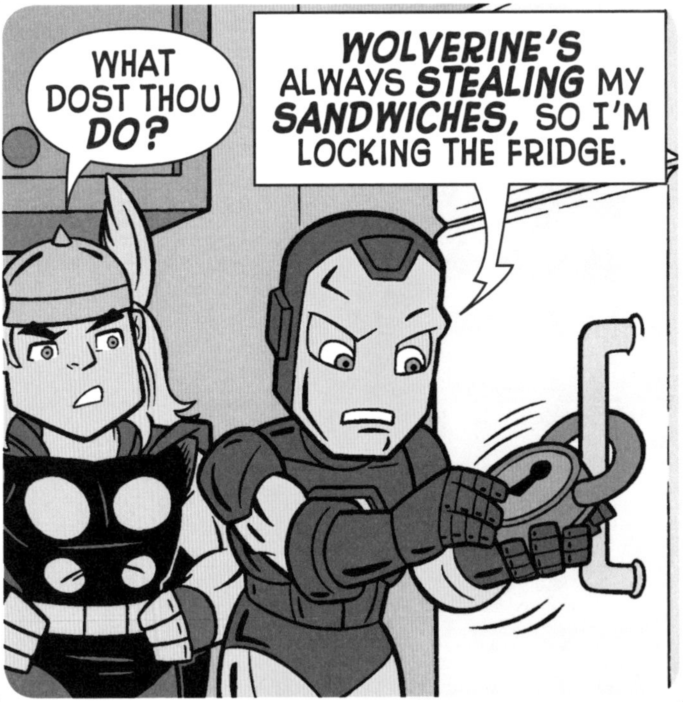
WHAT DOST THOU DO?
WOLVERINE'S ALWAYS STEALING MY SANDWICHES, SO I'M LOCKING THE FRIDGE.

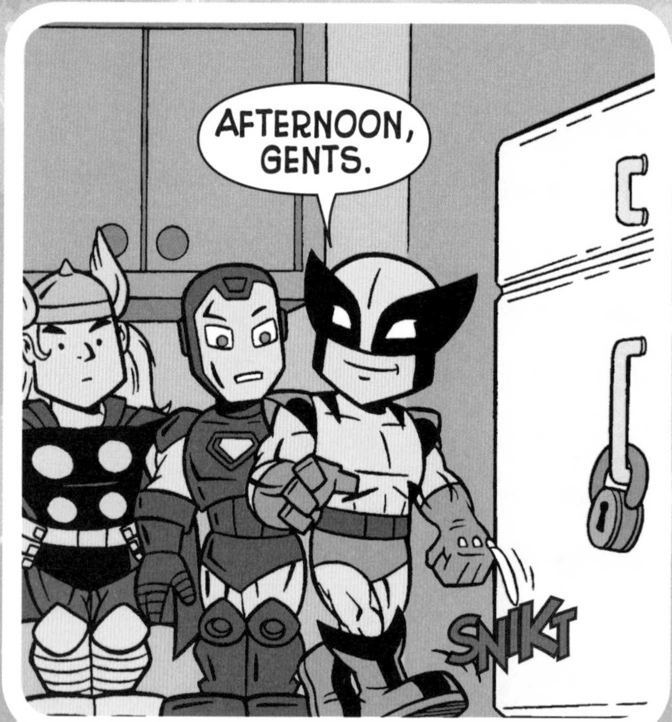
AFTERNOON, GENTS.
SNIKT

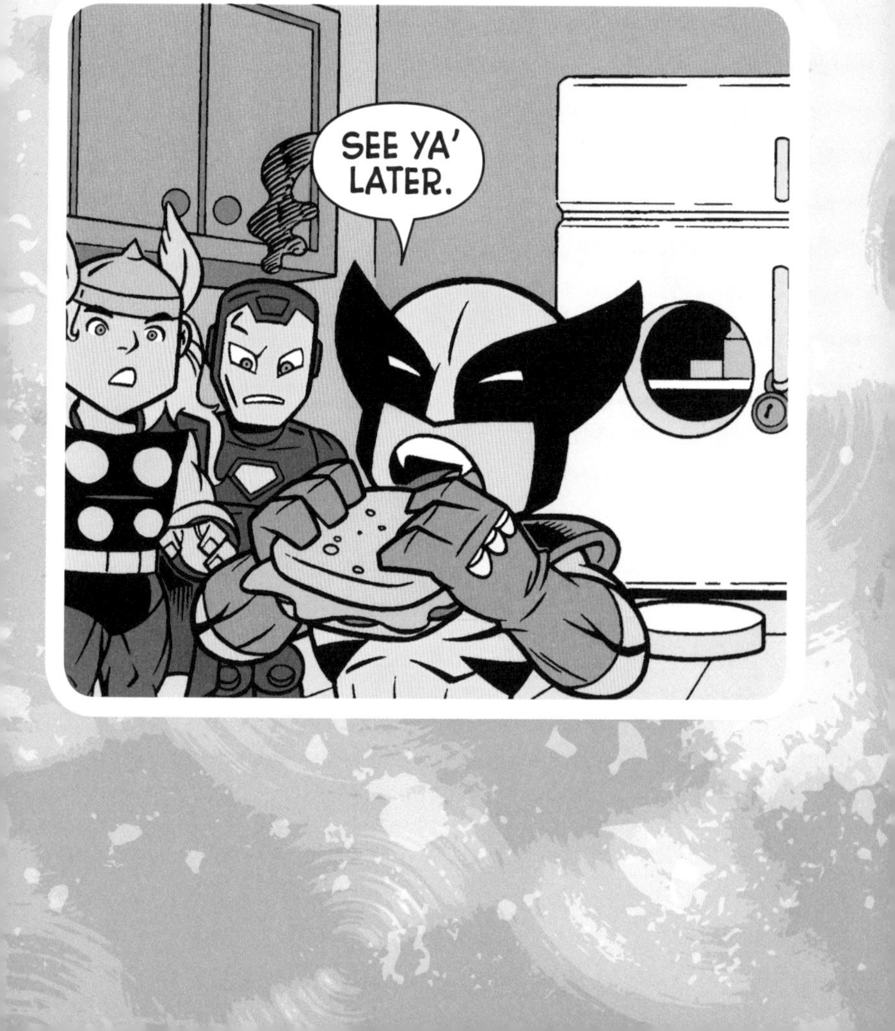
SEE YA'
LATER.

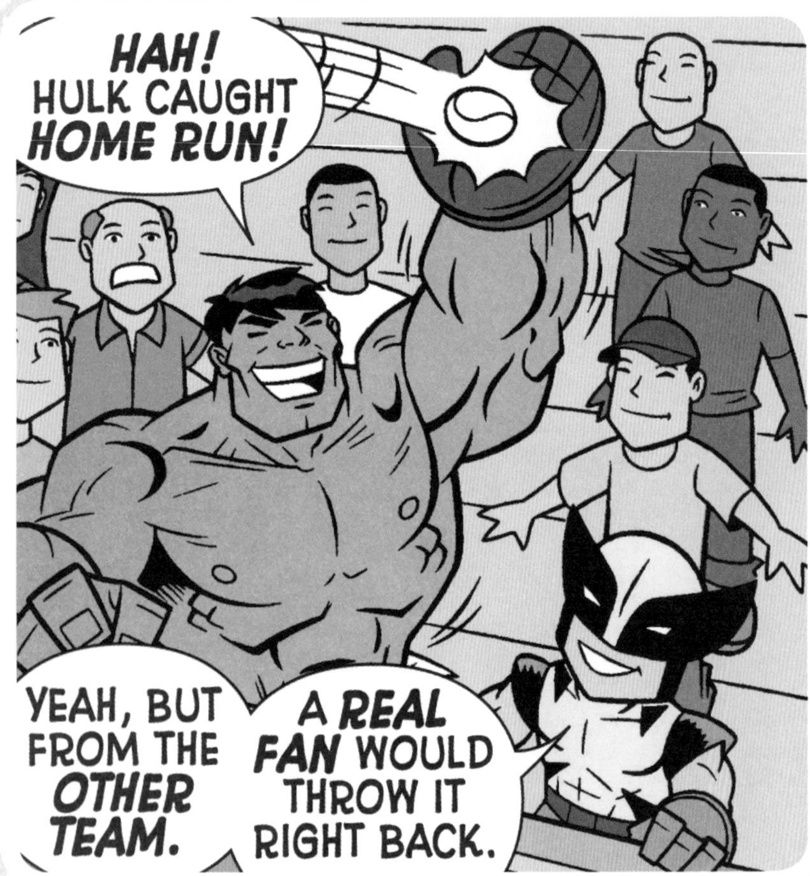
HAH! HULK CAUGHT HOME RUN!
YEAH, BUT FROM THE OTHER TEAM.
A REAL FAN WOULD THROW IT RIGHT BACK.

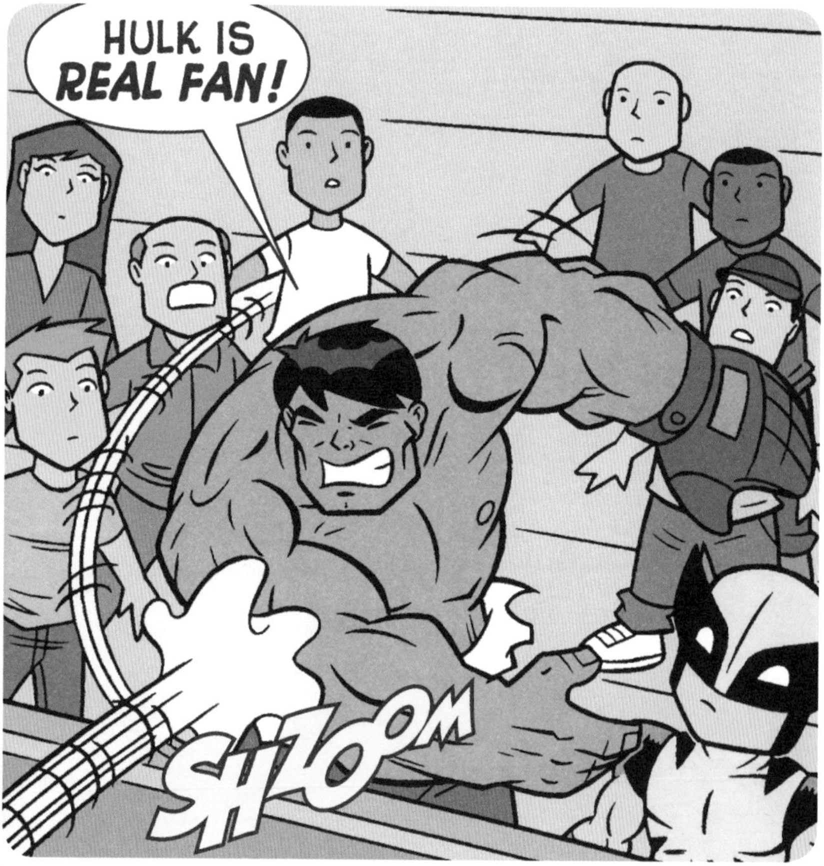
HULK IS
REAL FAN!
SHZOOM

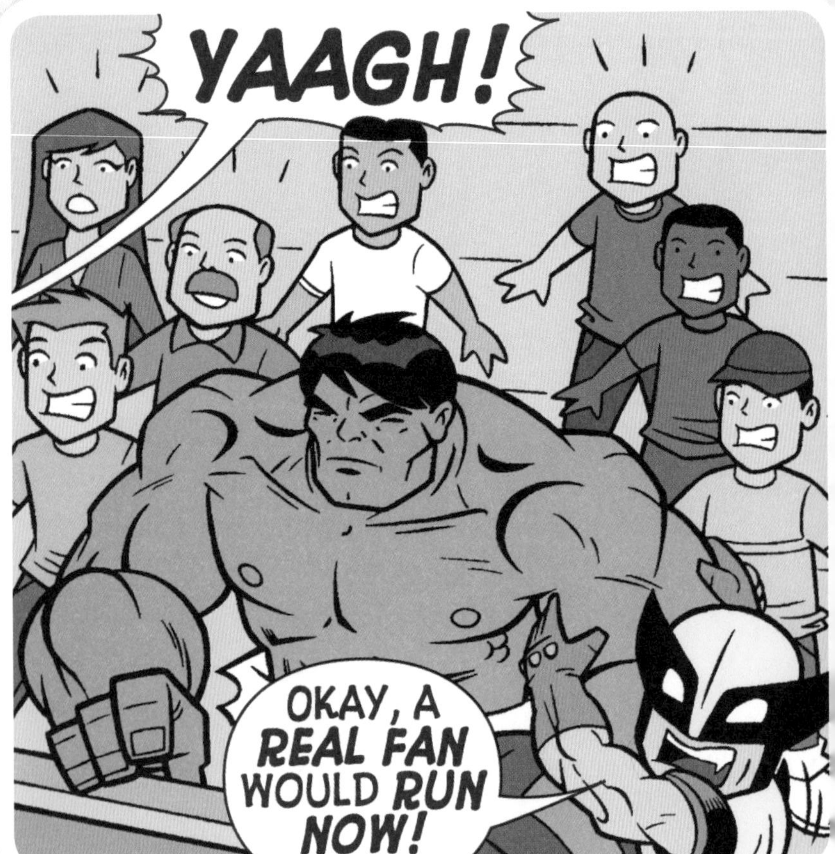
YAAGH!
OKAY, A REAL FAN WOULD RUN NOW!

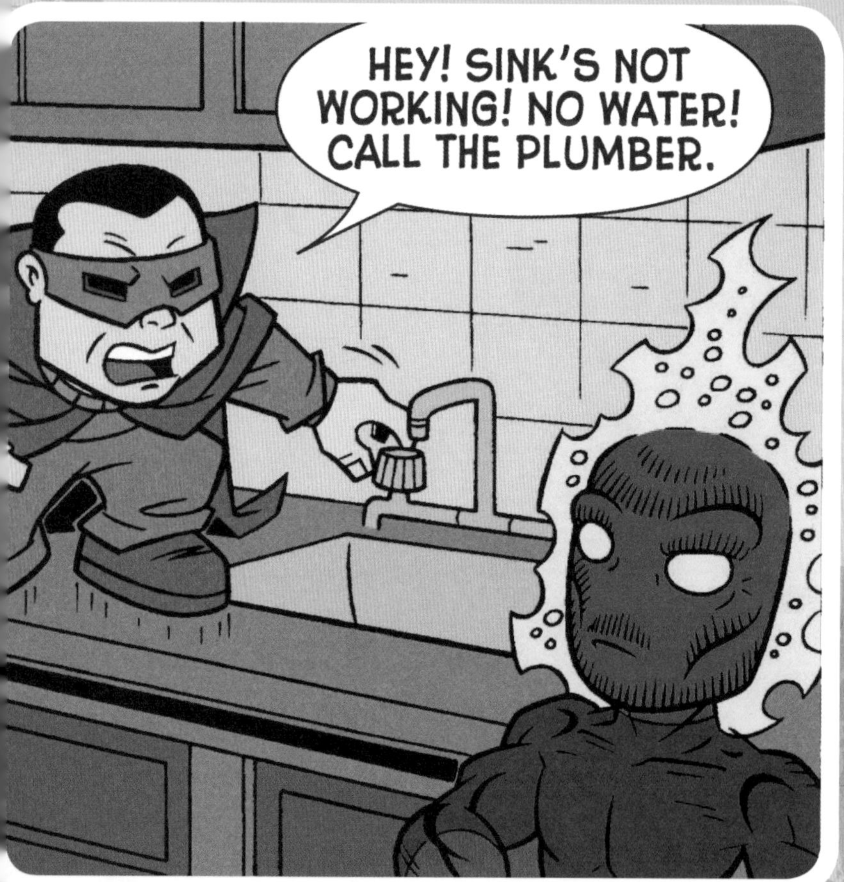
HEY! SINK'S NOT WORKING! NO WATER! CALL THE PLUMBER.

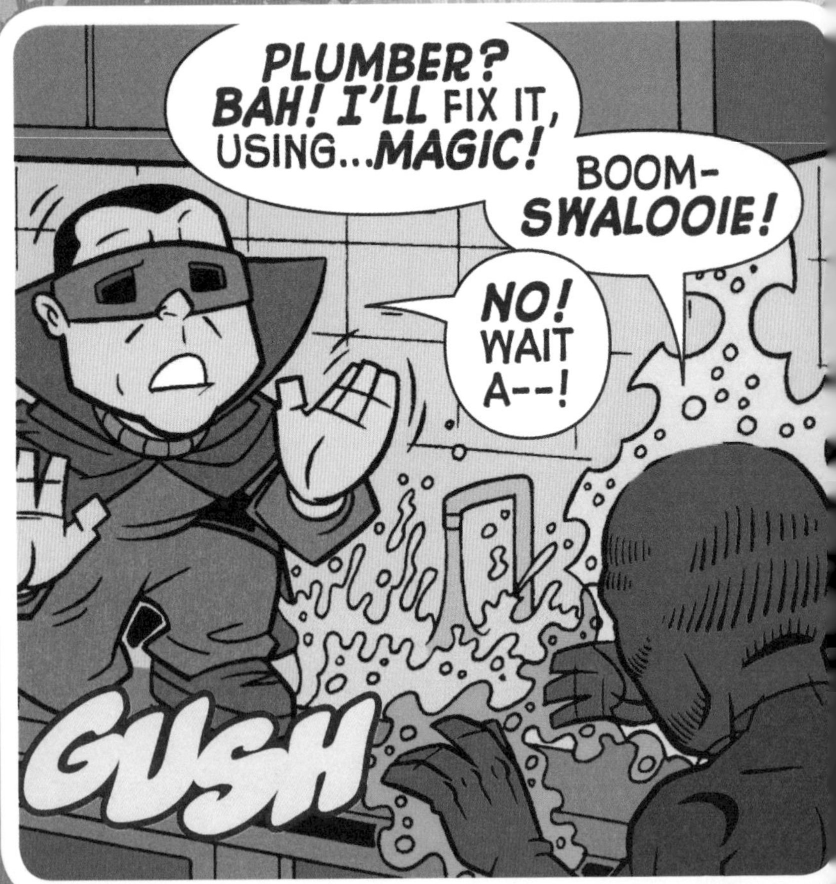
PLUMBER? BAH! I'LL FIX IT, USING...MAGIC!
BOOM-SWALOOIE!
NO! WAIT A--!
GUSH

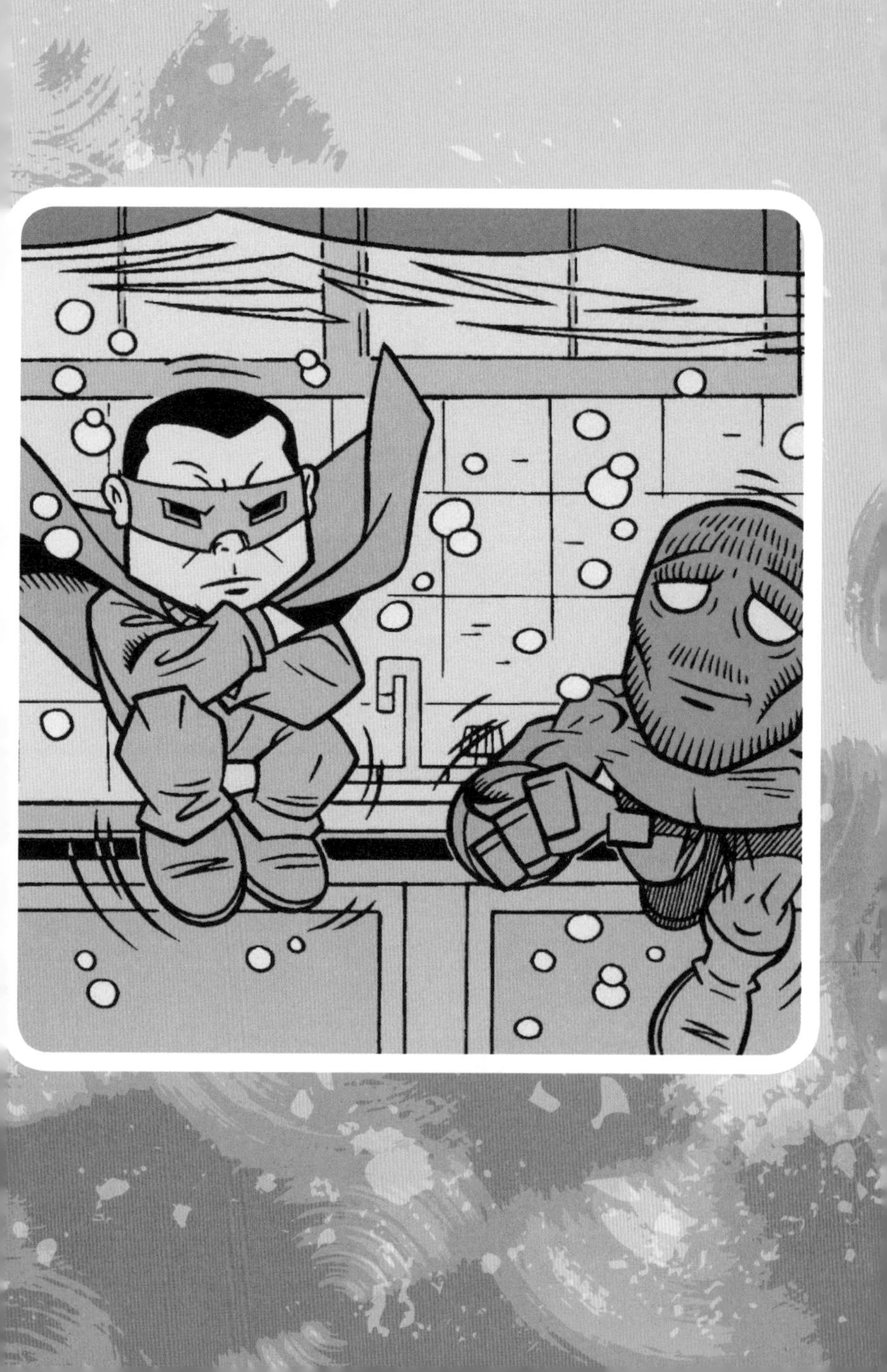

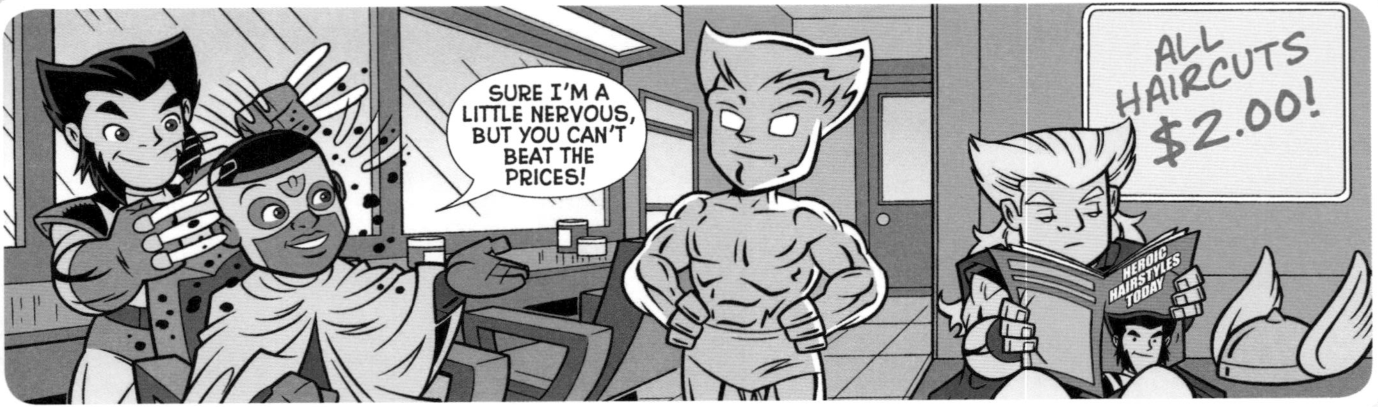
SURE I'M A LITTLE NERVOUS, BUT YOU CAN'T BEAT THE PRICES!
ALL HAIRCUTS $2.00!
HEROIC HAIRSTYLES TODAY

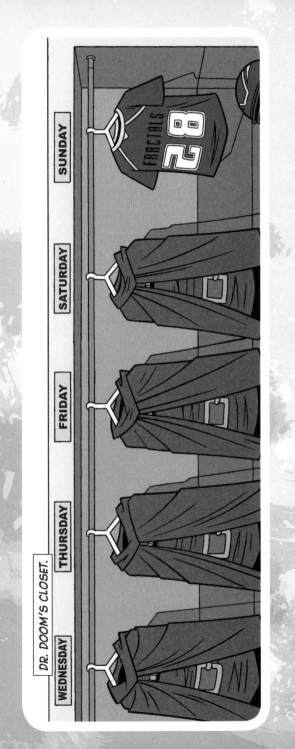

DR. DOOM'S CLOSET.

WEDNESDAY   THURSDAY   FRIDAY   SATURDAY   SUNDAY

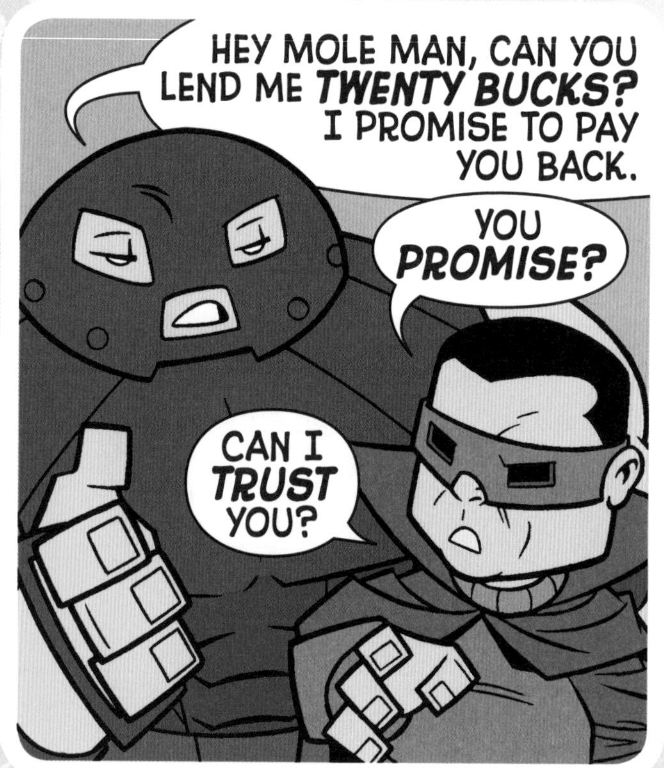
HEY MOLE MAN, CAN YOU LEND ME TWENTY BUCKS? I PROMISE TO PAY YOU BACK.
YOU PROMISE?
CAN I TRUST YOU?

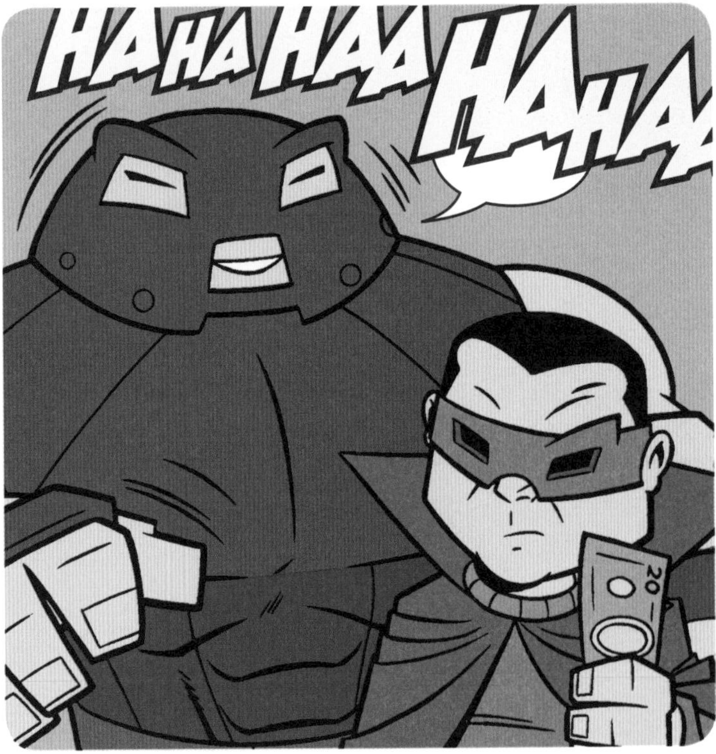

HA HA HAA HAHA
20

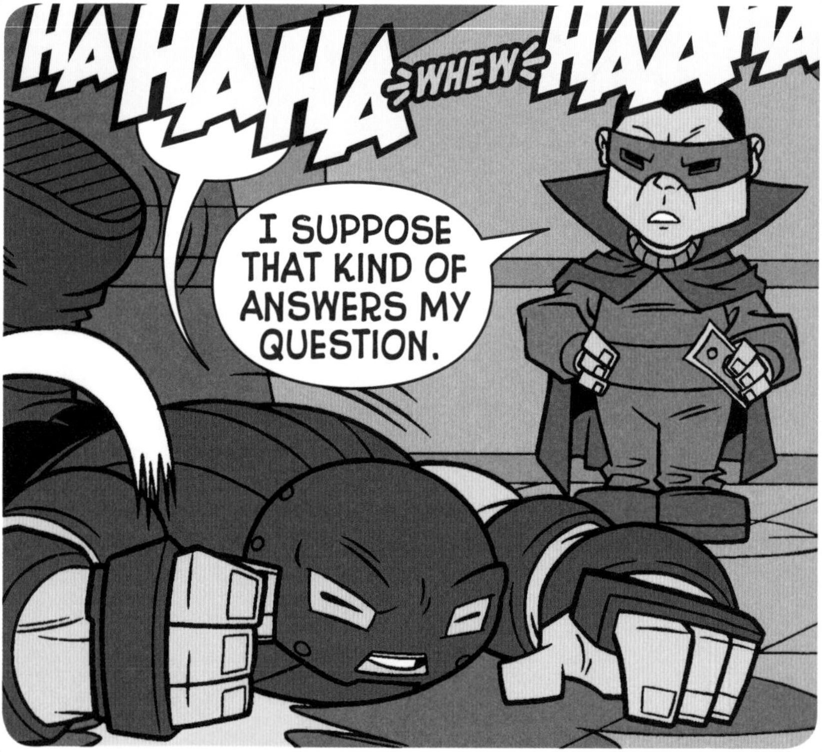
HAHAHAHA
WHEW
HAHAHA
I SUPPOSE THAT KIND OF ANSWERS MY QUESTION.

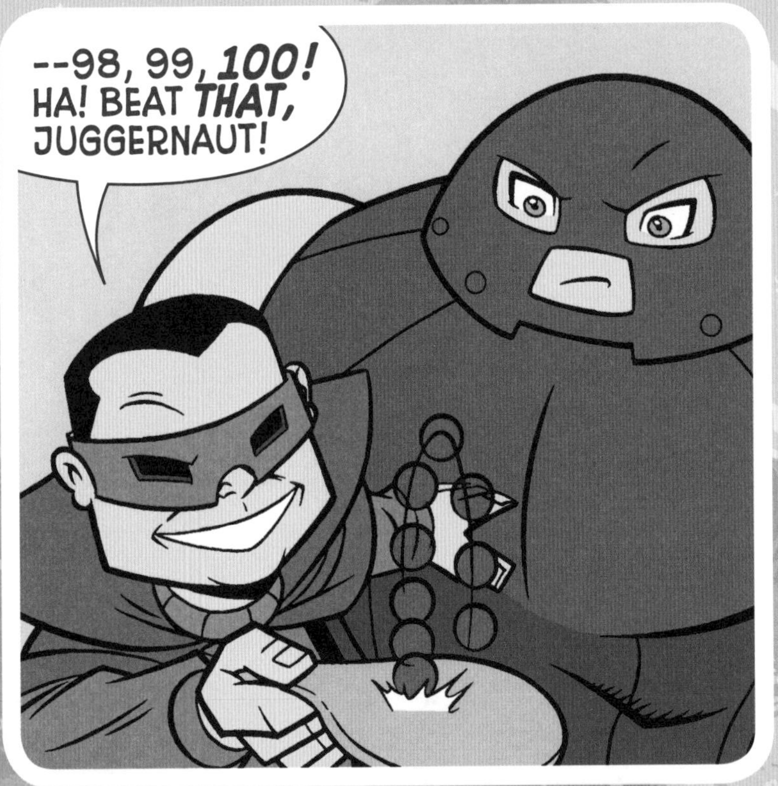
--98, 99, 100! HA! BEAT THAT, JUGGERNAUT!

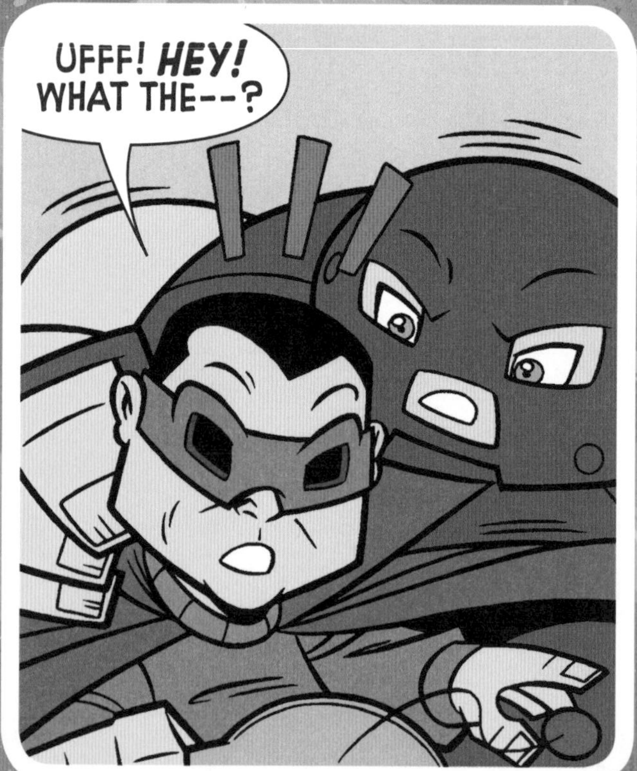
UFFF! HEY! WHAT THE--?

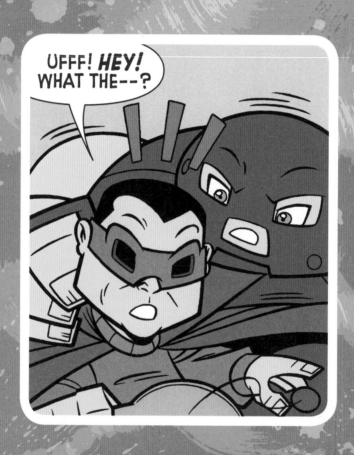

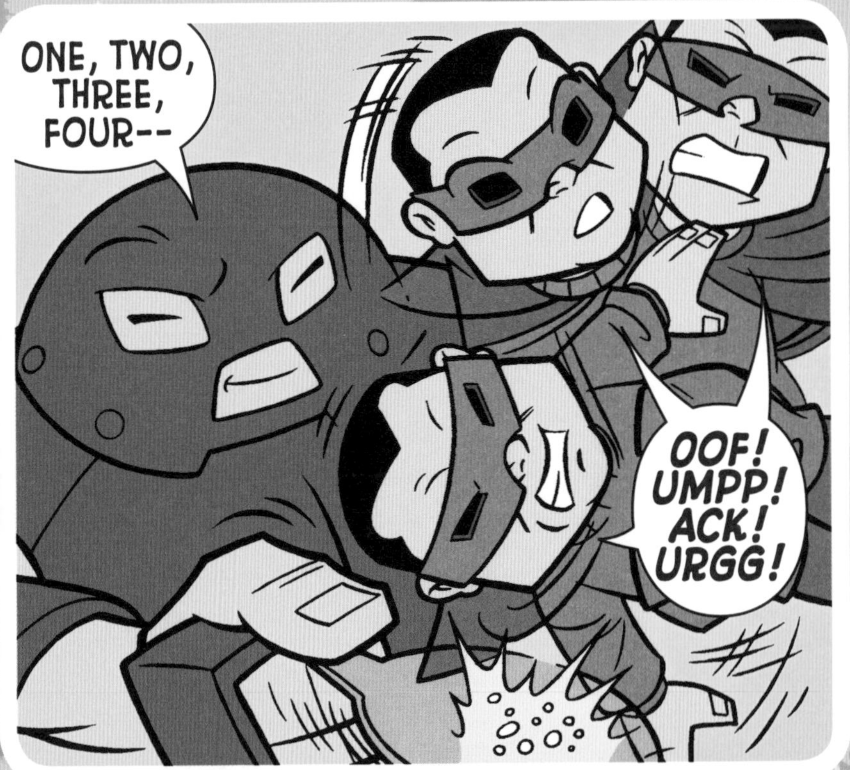
ONE, TWO, THREE, FOUR--
OOF! UMPP! ACK! URGG!

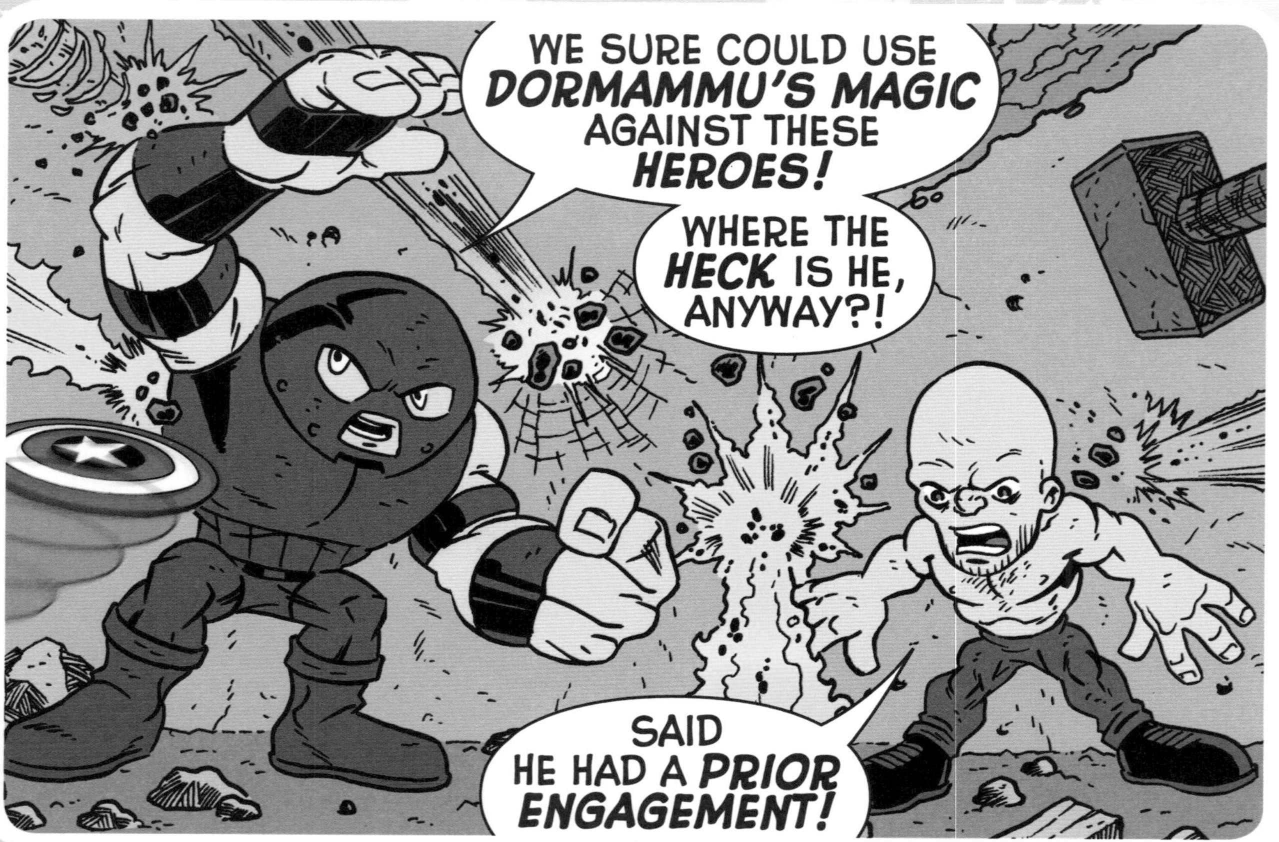
WE SURE COULD USE ***DORMAMMU'S MAGIC*** AGAINST THESE ***HEROES!***
WHERE THE ***HECK*** IS HE, ANYWAY?!
SAID HE HAD A ***PRIOR ENGAGEMENT!***

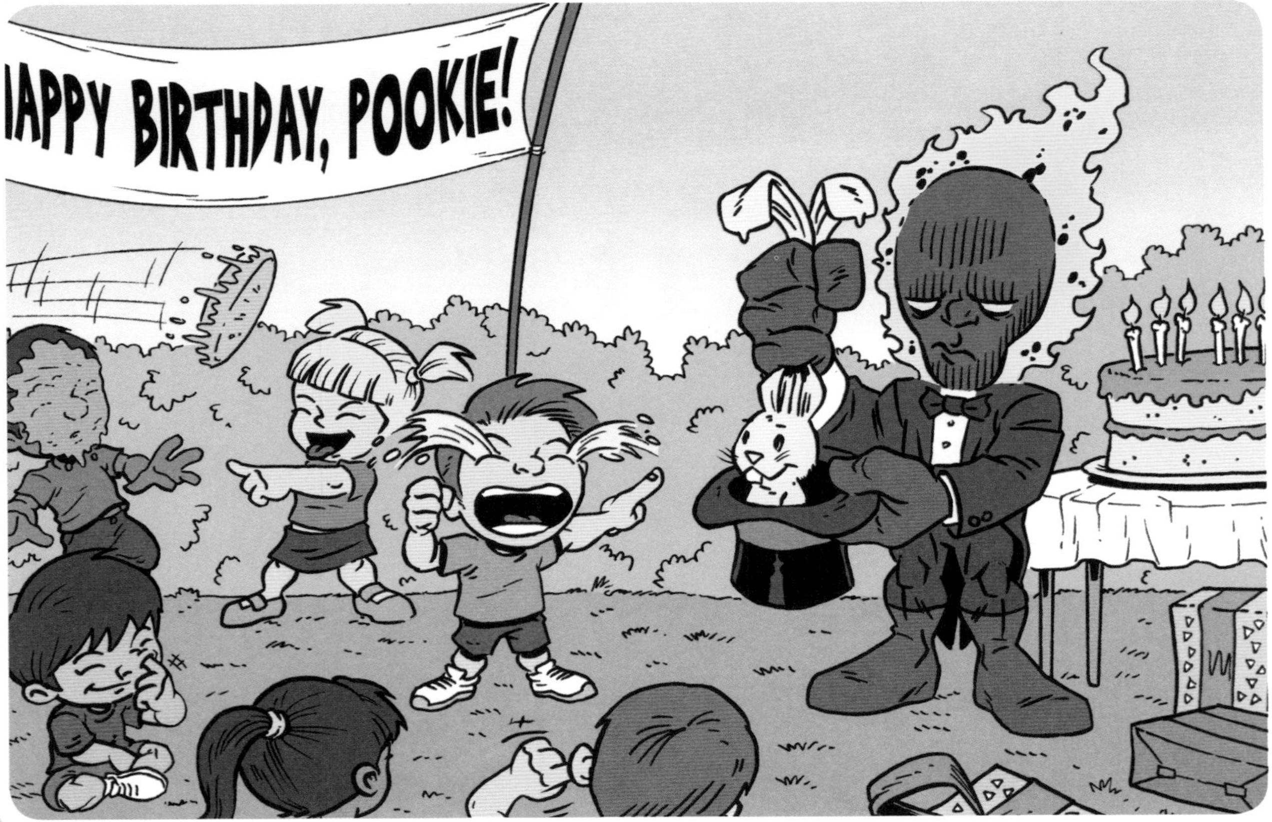

IAPPY BIRTHDAY, POOKIE!

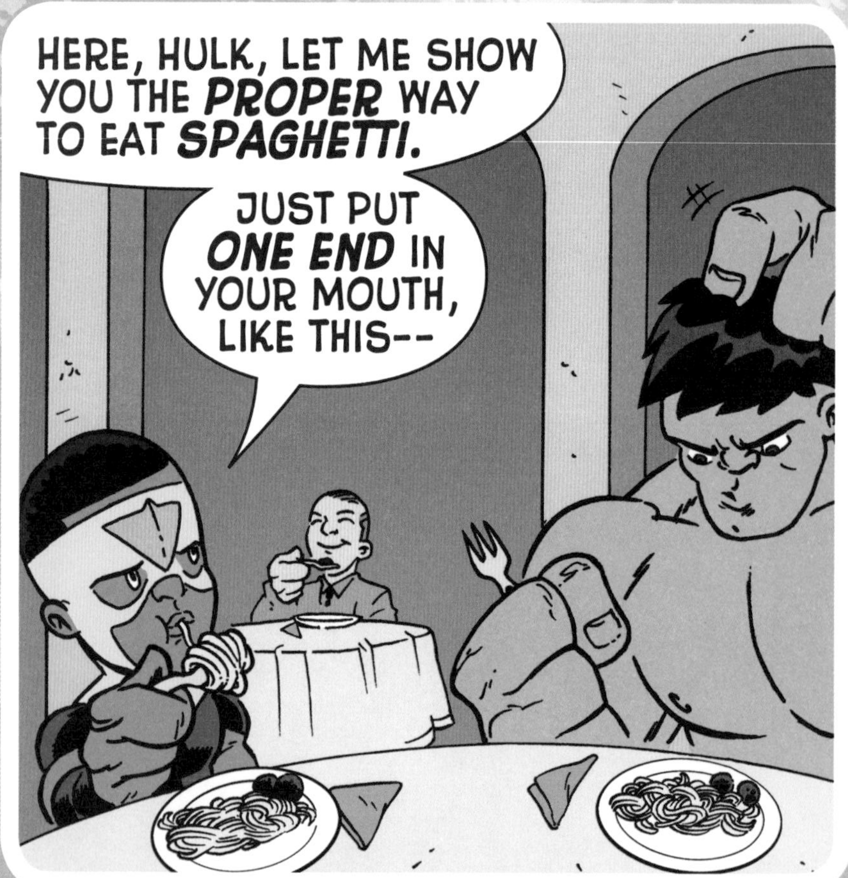
HERE, HULK, LET ME SHOW YOU THE *PROPER* WAY TO EAT *SPAGHETTI.*
JUST PUT *ONE END* IN YOUR MOUTH, LIKE THIS--

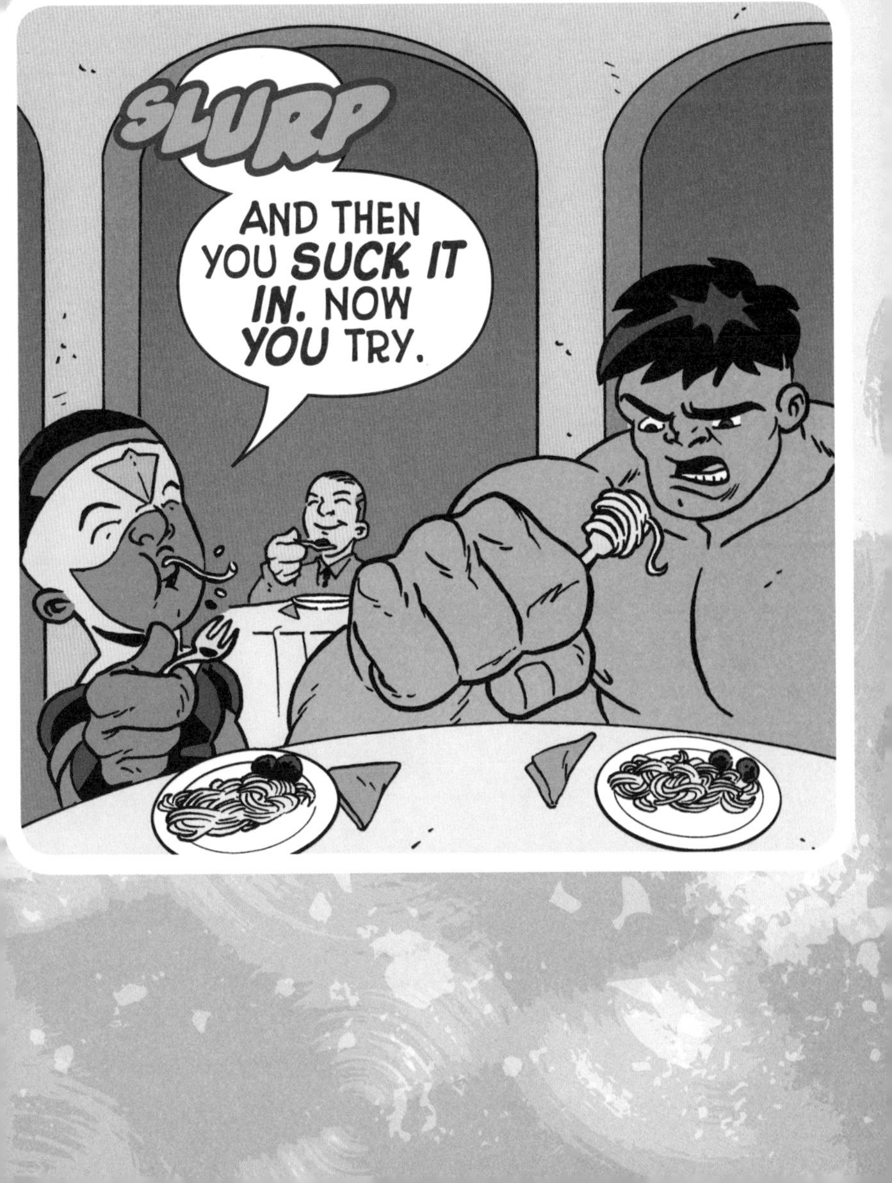
SLURP
AND THEN YOU SUCK IT IN. NOW YOU TRY.

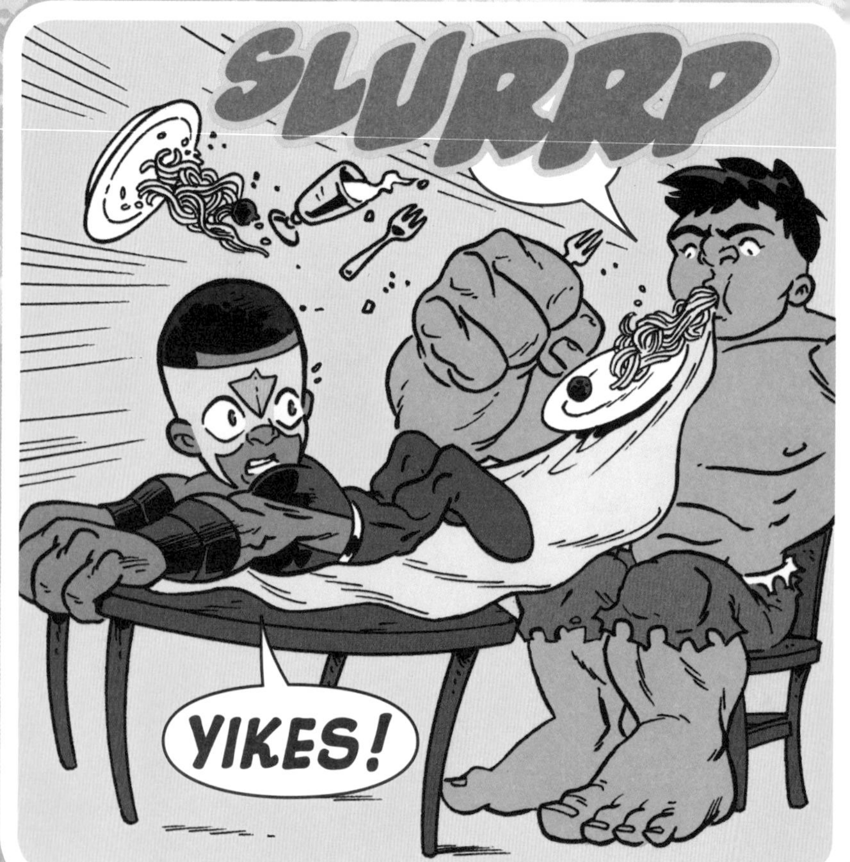
SLURRP
YIKES!

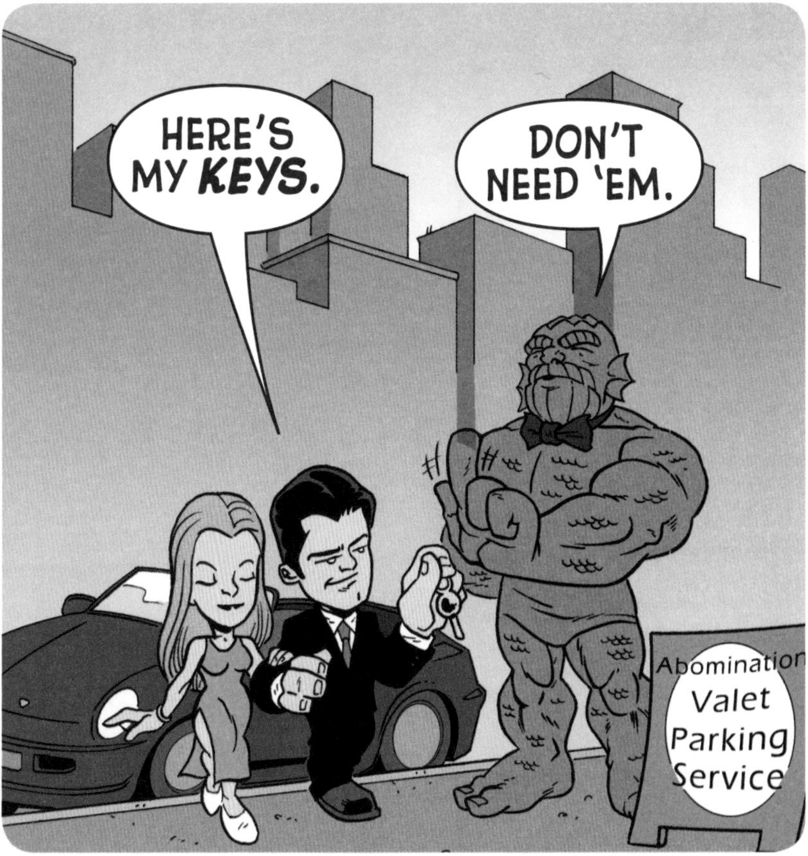
HERE'S MY KEYS.
DON'T NEED 'EM.
Abominatio
Valet
Parking
Service

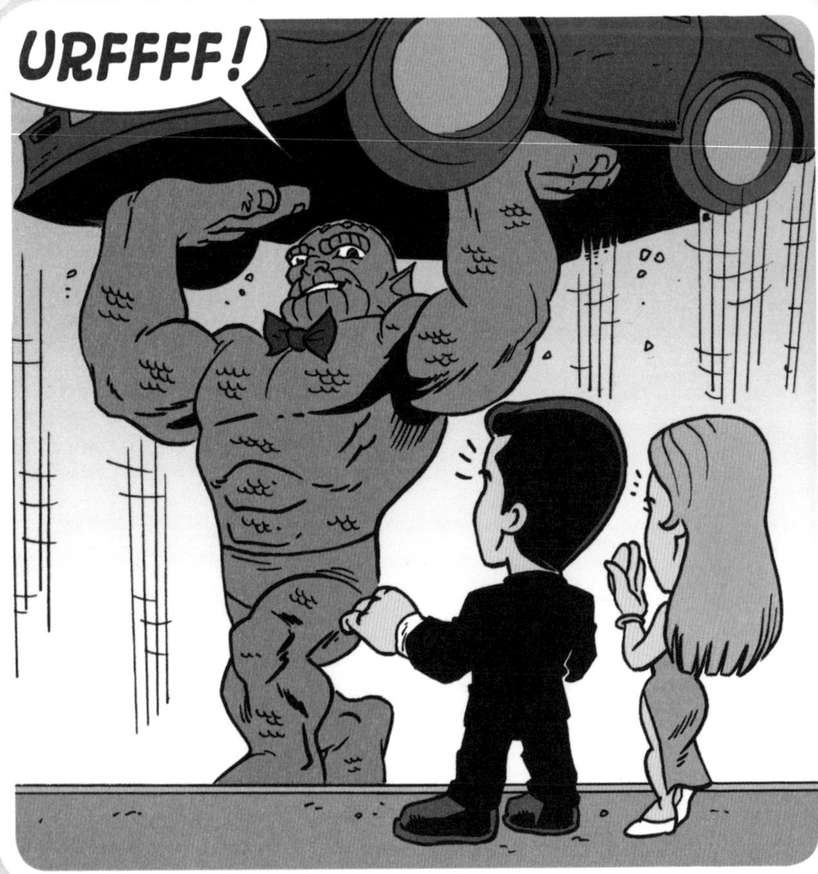
URFFFF!

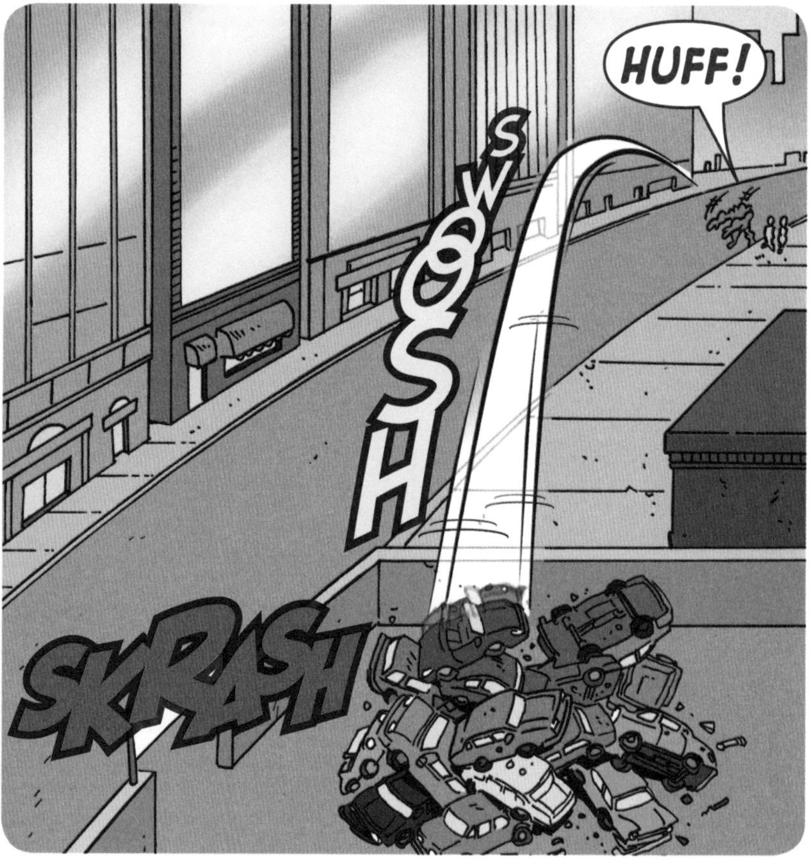
HUFF!
SWOOSH
SKRASH

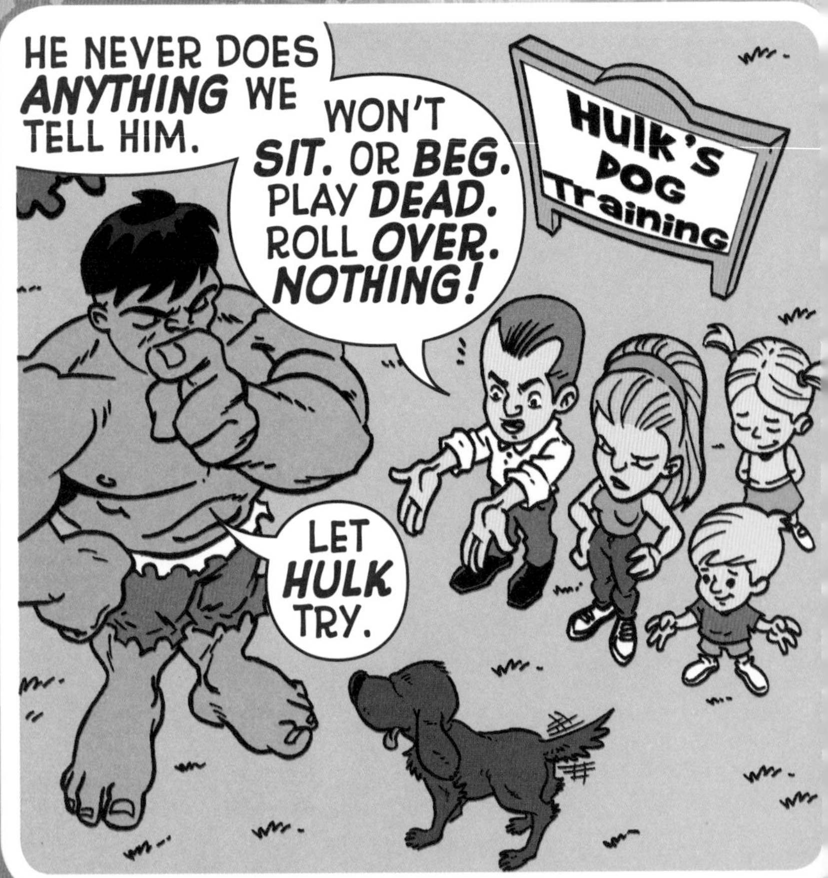

HE NEVER DOES ANYTHING WE TELL HIM.
WON'T SIT. OR BEG. PLAY DEAD. ROLL OVER. NOTHING!
Hulk's DOG Training
LET HULK TRY.

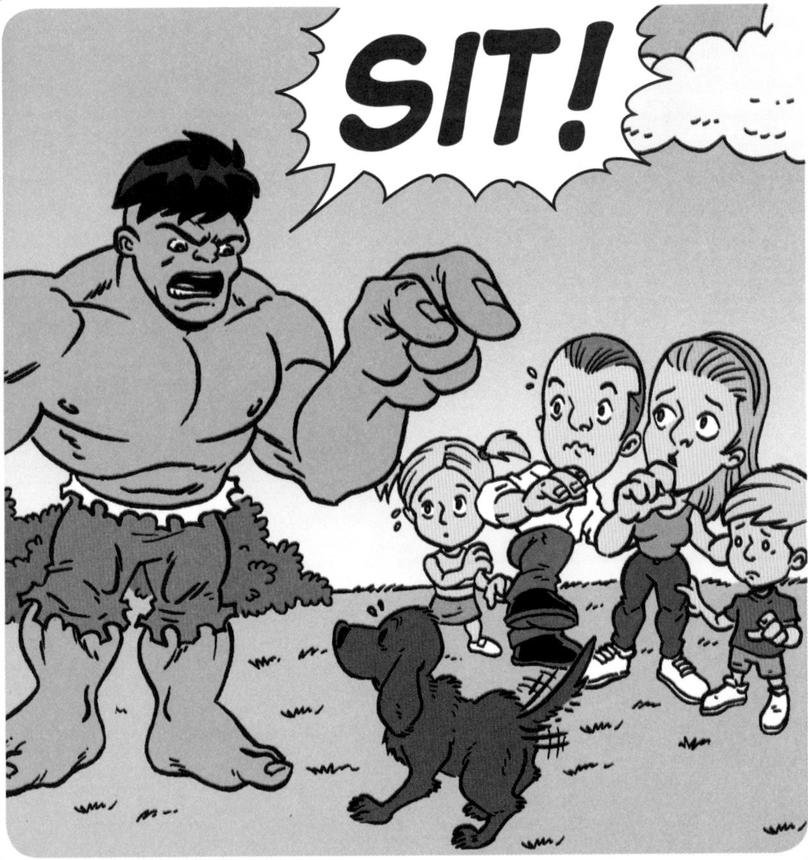
SIT!

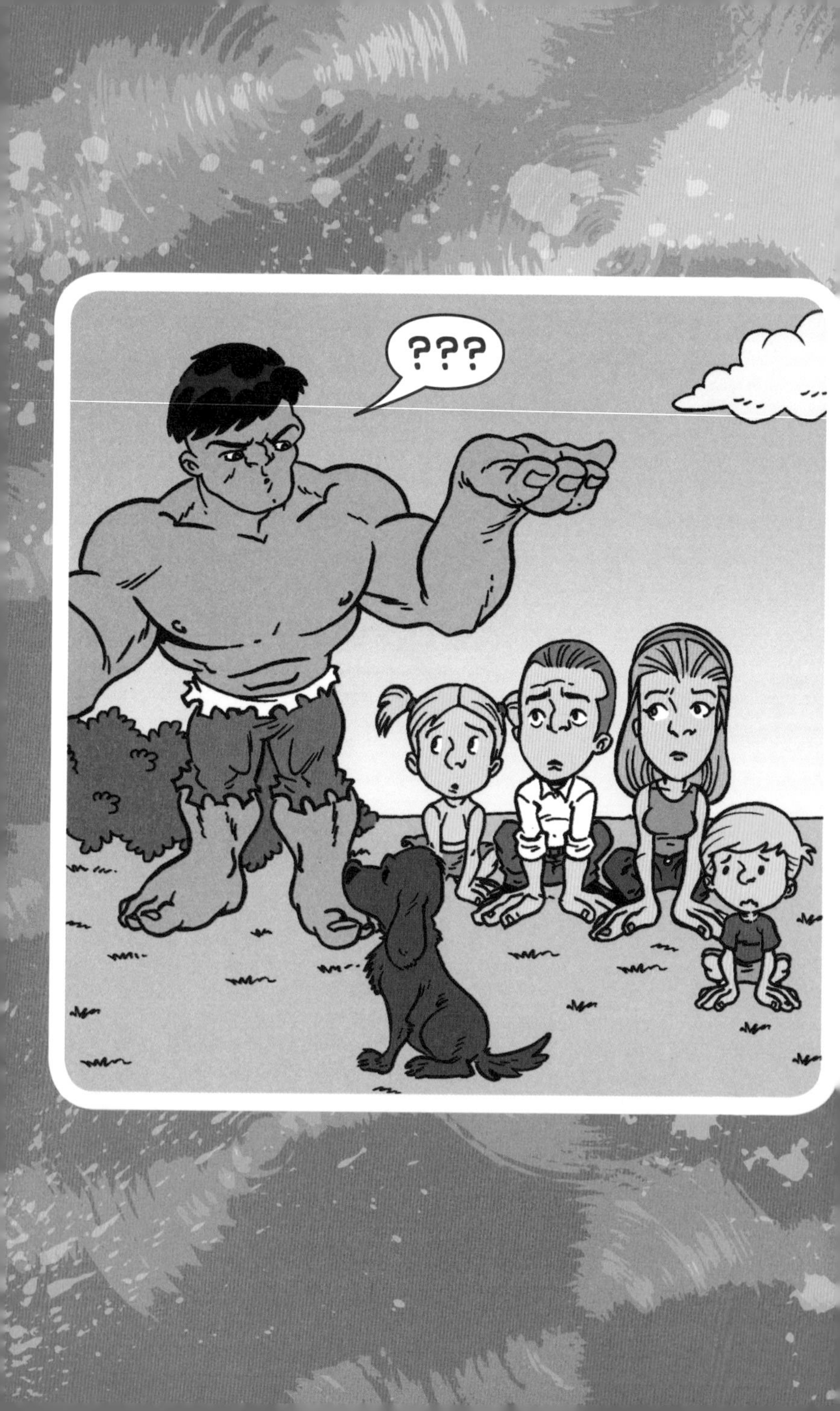
???

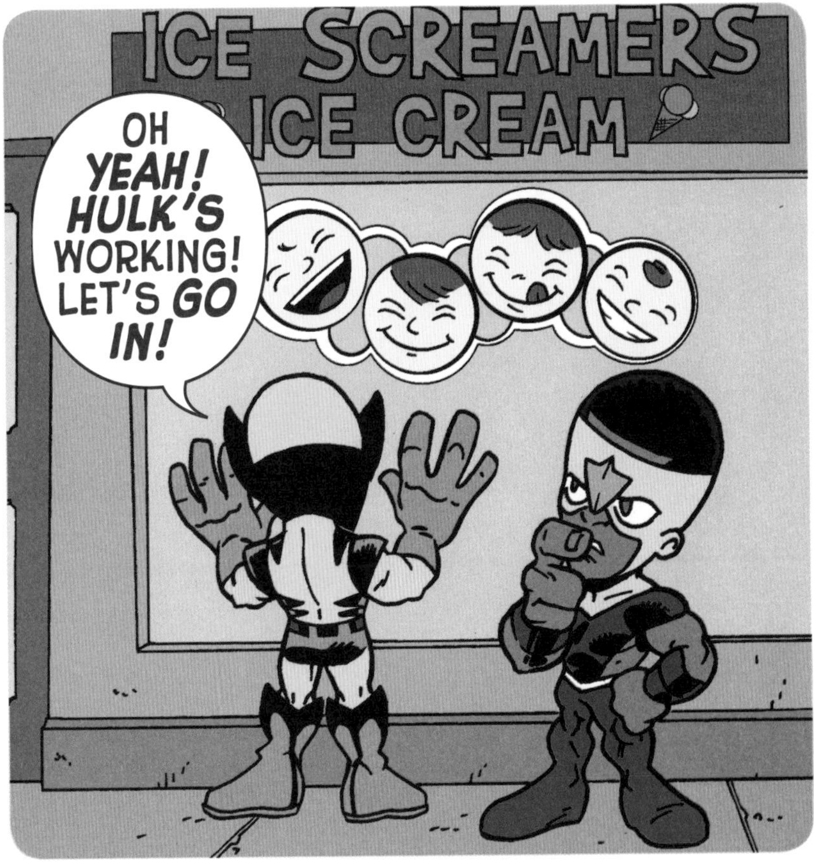
ICE SCREAMERS
ICE CREAM
OH YEAH! HULK'S WORKING! LET'S GO IN!

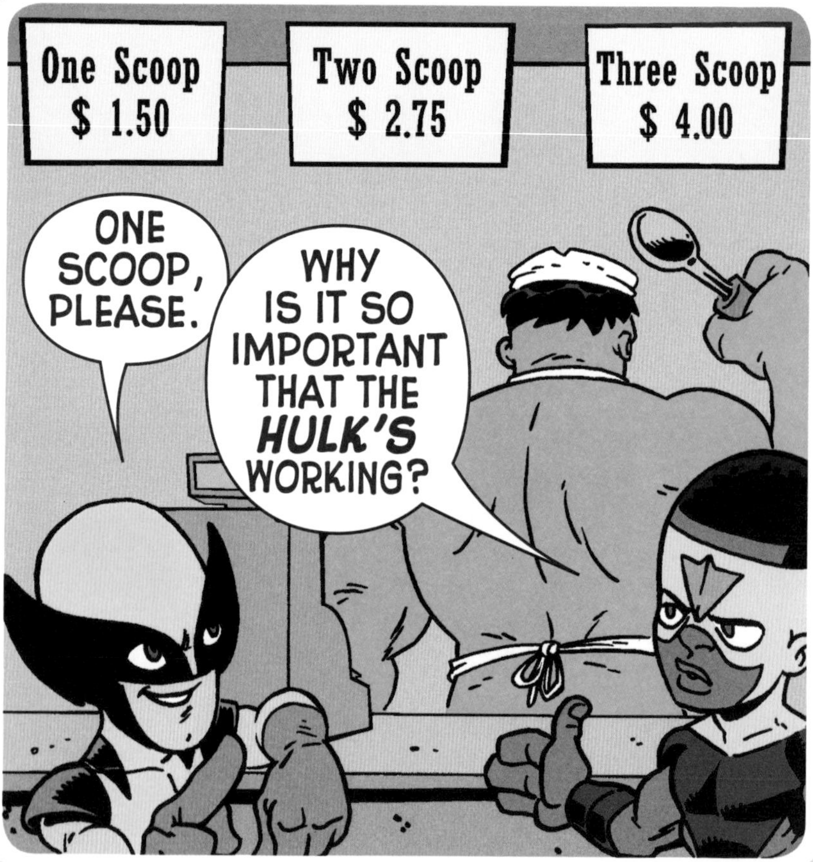
One Scoop $ 1.50
Two Scoop $ 2.75
Three Scoop $ 4.00
ONE SCOOP, PLEASE.
WHY IS IT SO IMPORTANT THAT THE ***HULK'S*** WORKING?

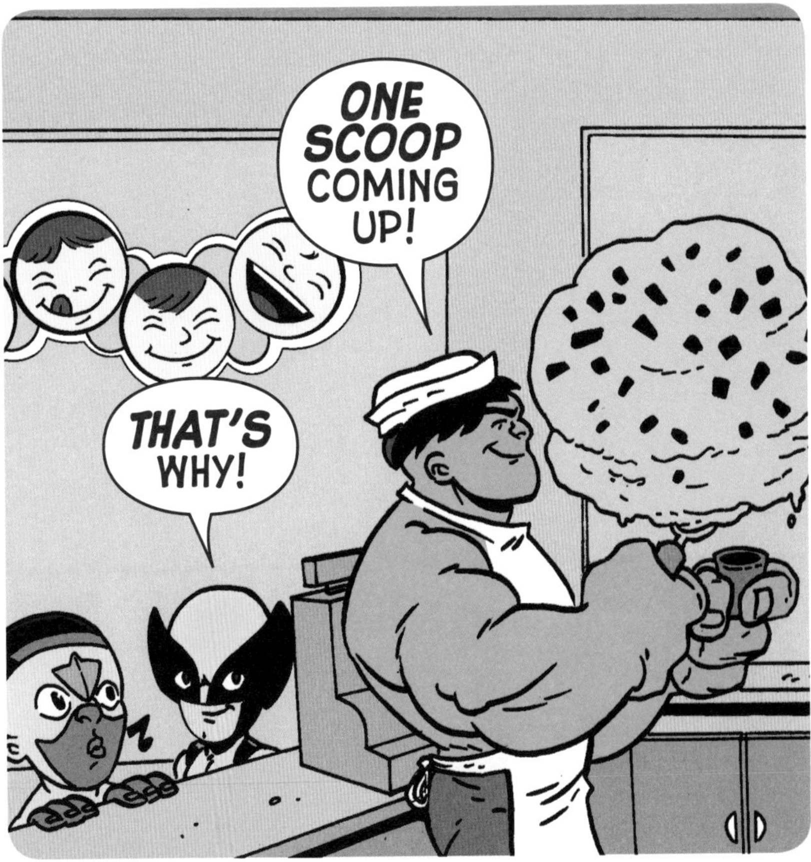

ONE SCOOP COMING UP!
THAT'S WHY!

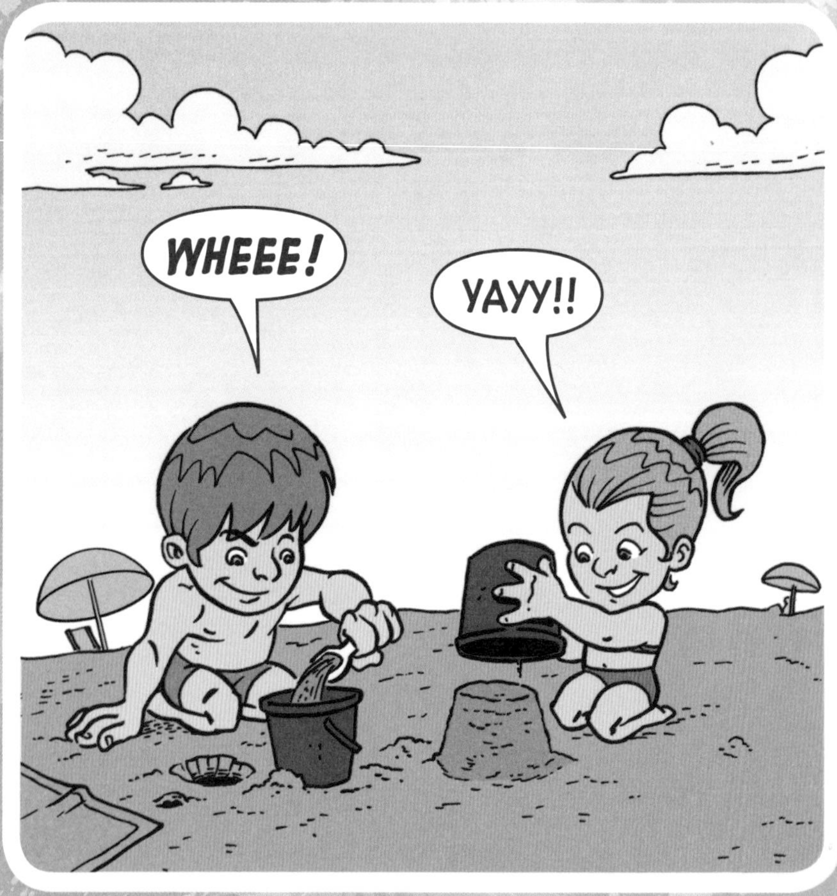
WHEEE!
YAYY!!

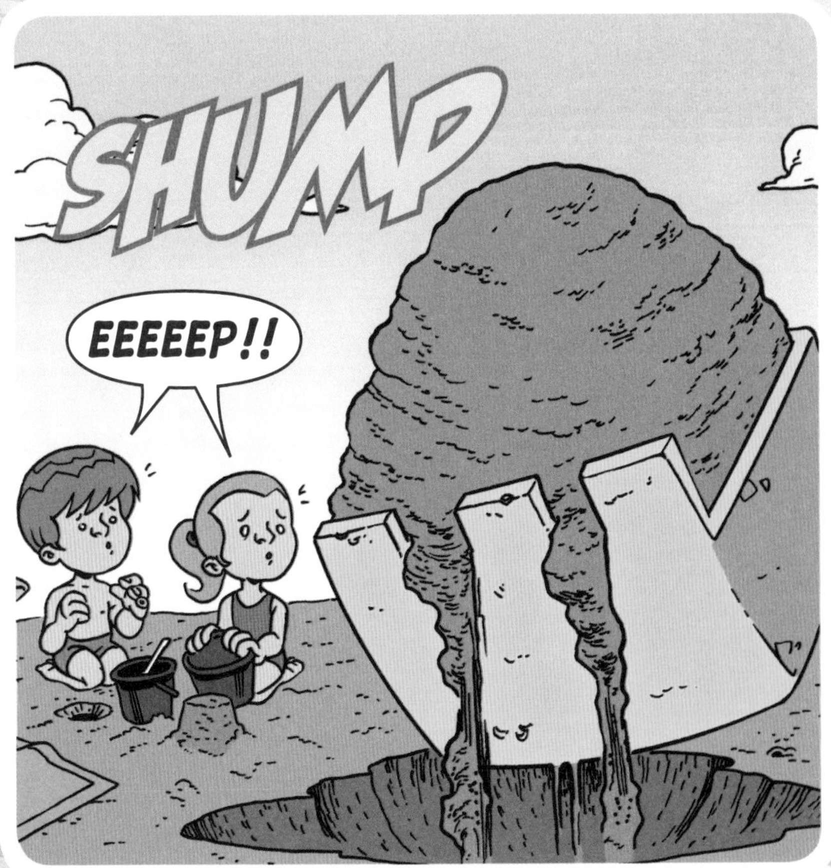
SHUMP
EEEEEP!!

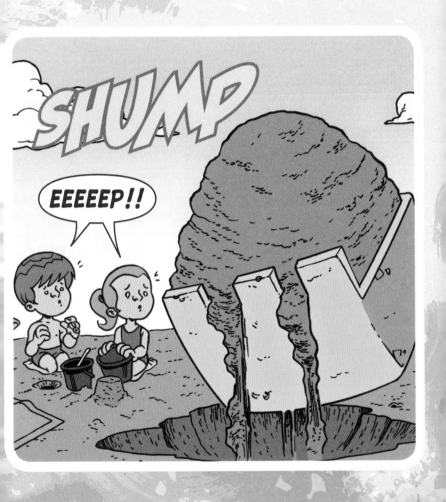

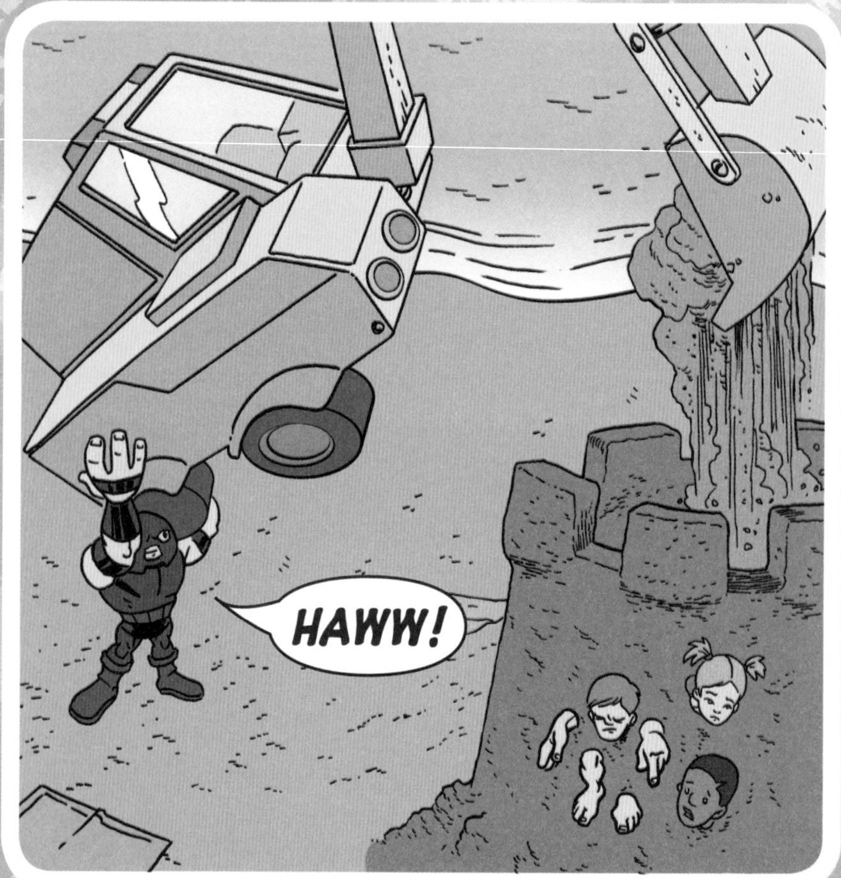
HAWW!

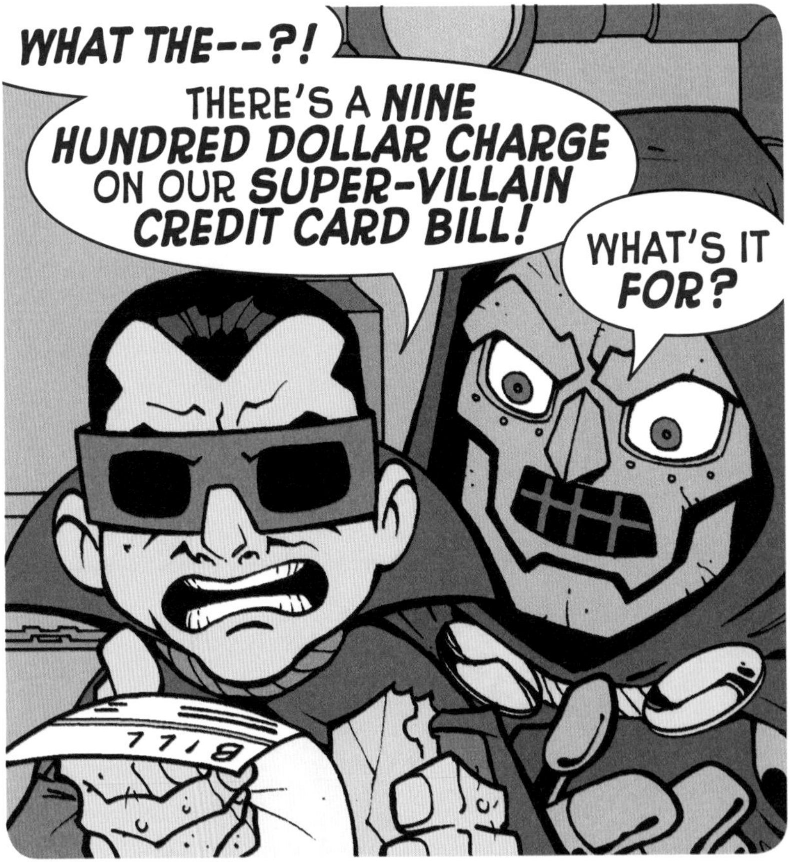
WHAT THE--?!
THERE'S A NINE HUNDRED DOLLAR CHARGE ON OUR SUPER-VILLAIN CREDIT CARD BILL!
WHAT'S IT FOR?
BILL

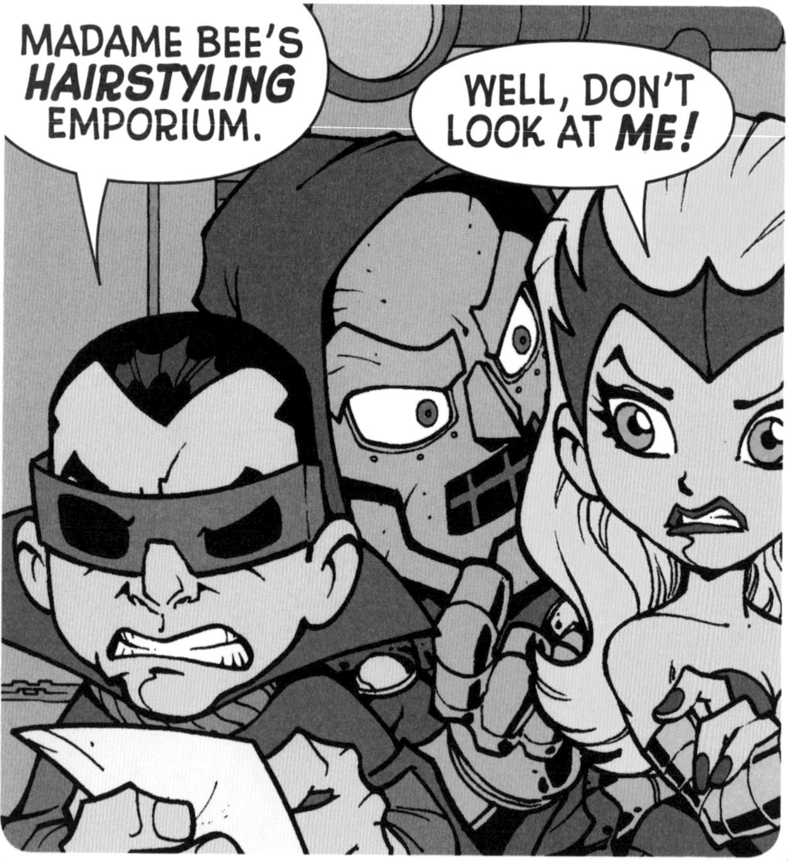
MADAME BEE'S **HAIRSTYLING** EMPORIUM.
WELL, DON'T LOOK AT **ME!**

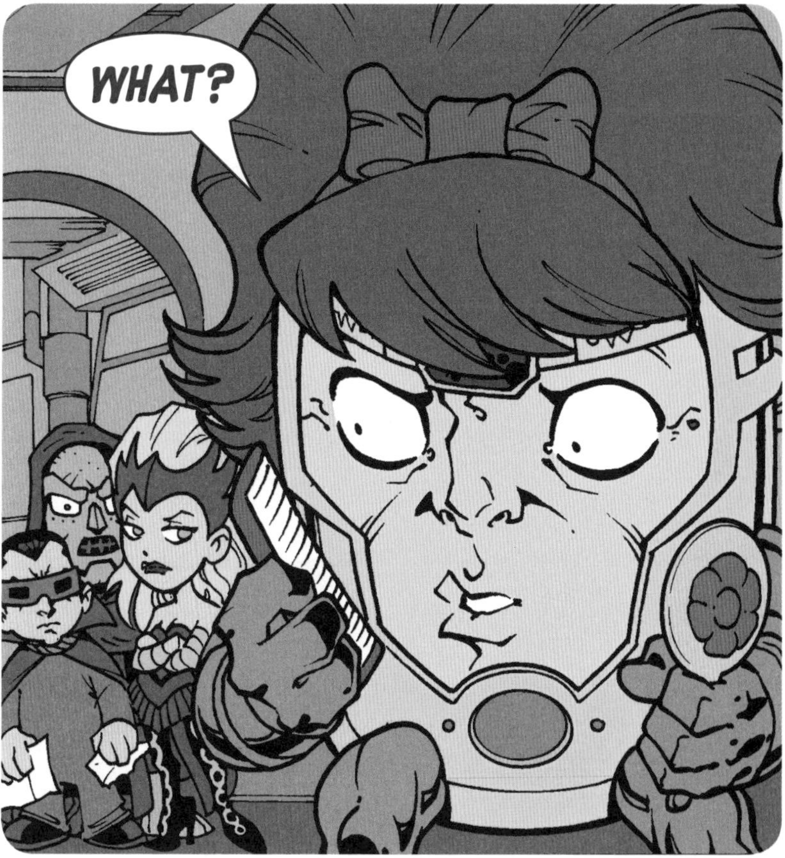
WHAT?

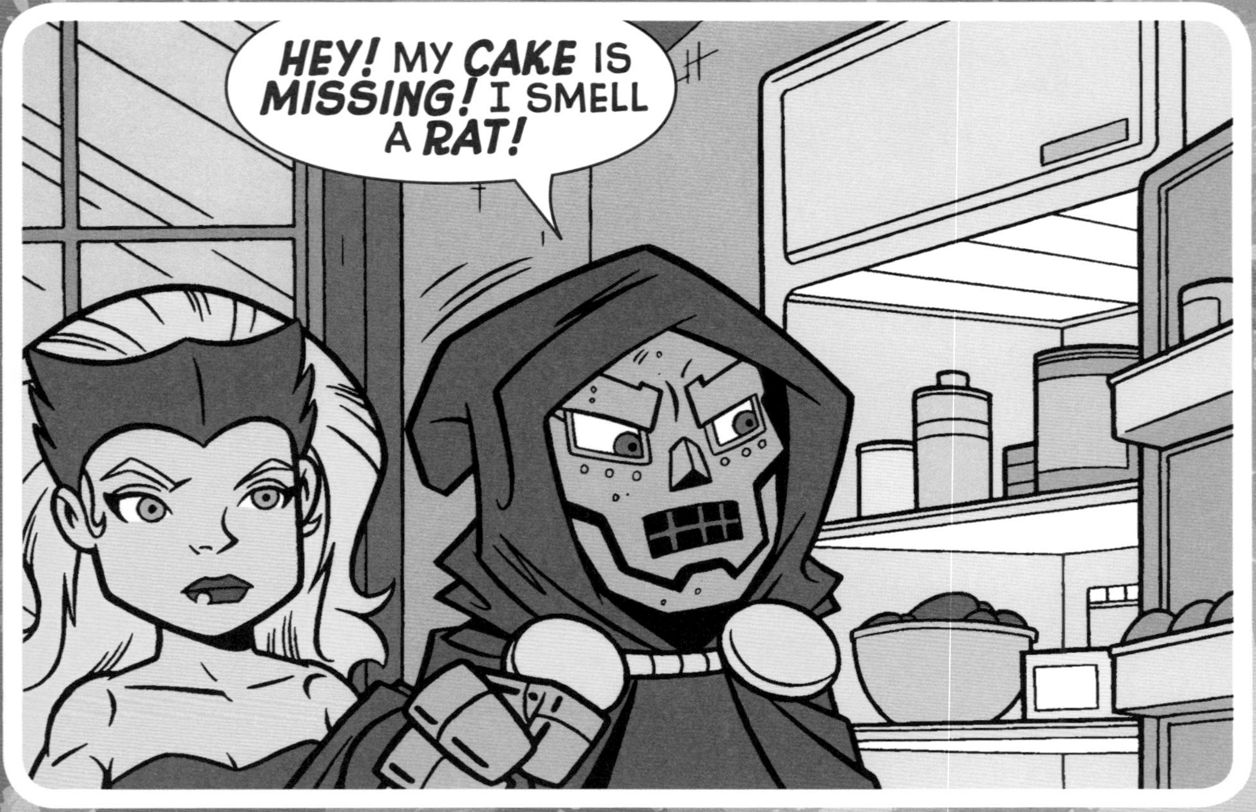
HEY! MY CAKE IS MISSING! I SMELL A RAT!

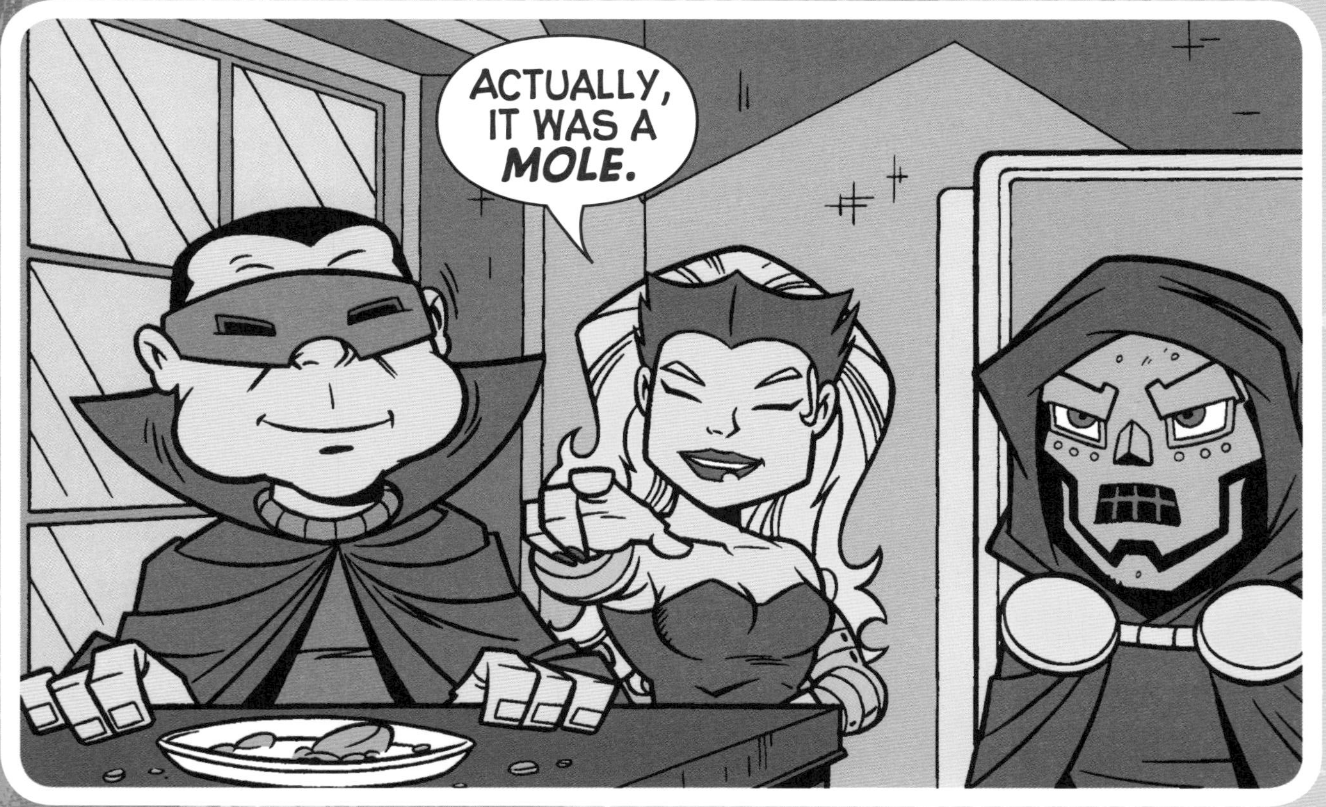
ACTUALLY, IT WAS A *MOLE.*

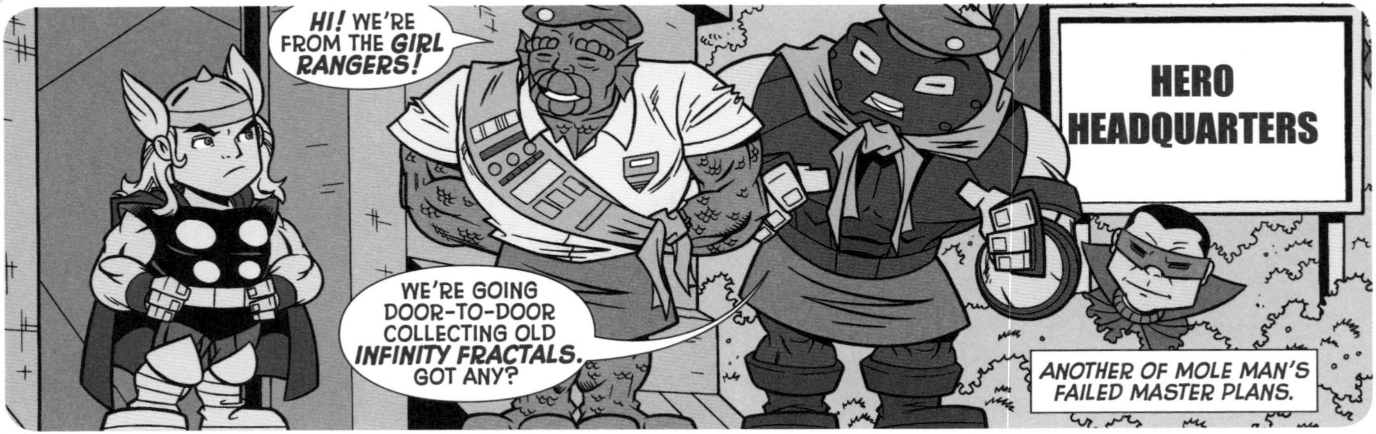
HI! WE'RE FROM THE GIRL RANGERS!
WE'RE GOING DOOR-TO-DOOR COLLECTING OLD INFINITY FRACTALS. GOT ANY?
HERO HEADQUARTERS
ANOTHER OF MOLE MAN'S FAILED MASTER PLANS.

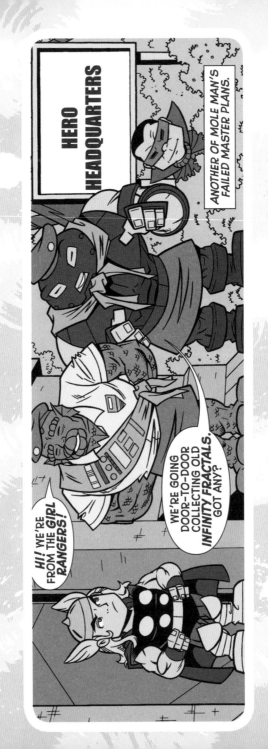

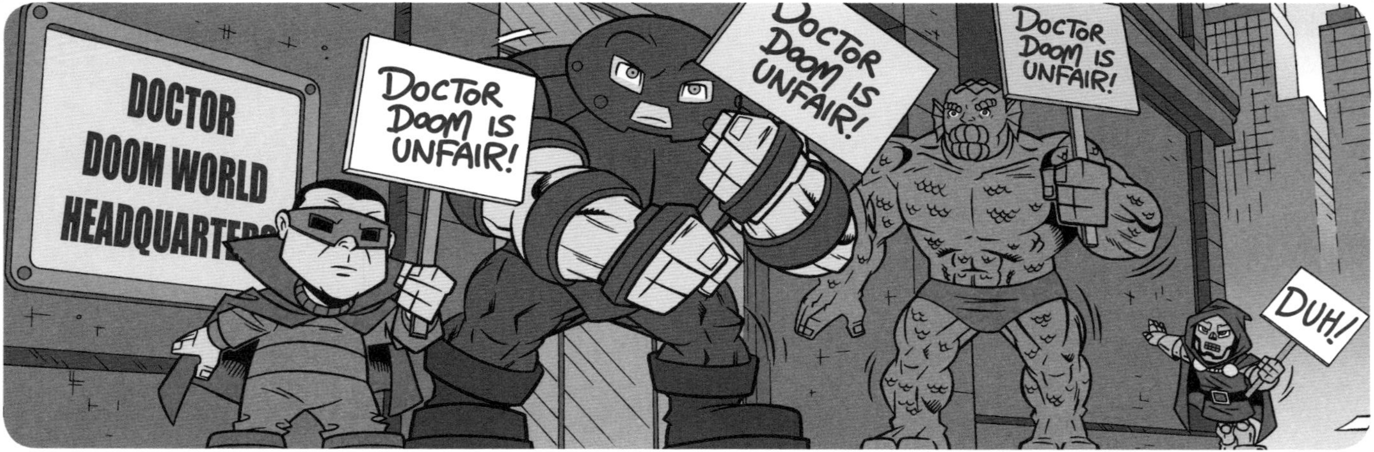
DOCTOR DOOM WORLD HEADQUARTERS
DOCTOR DOOM IS UNFAIR!
DOCTOR DOOM IS UNFAIR!
DOCTOR DOOM IS UNFAIR!
DUH!

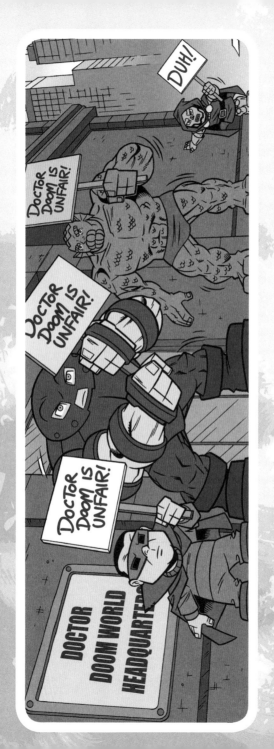

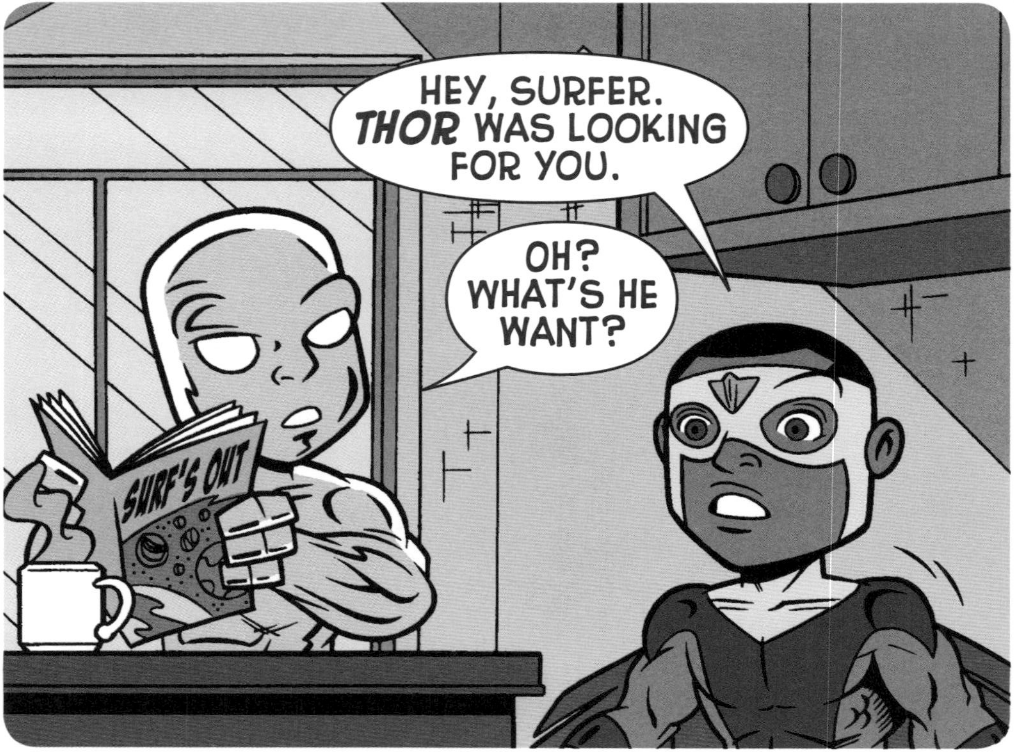
HEY, SURFER. **THOR** WAS LOOKING FOR YOU.
OH? WHAT'S HE WANT?
SURF'S OUT

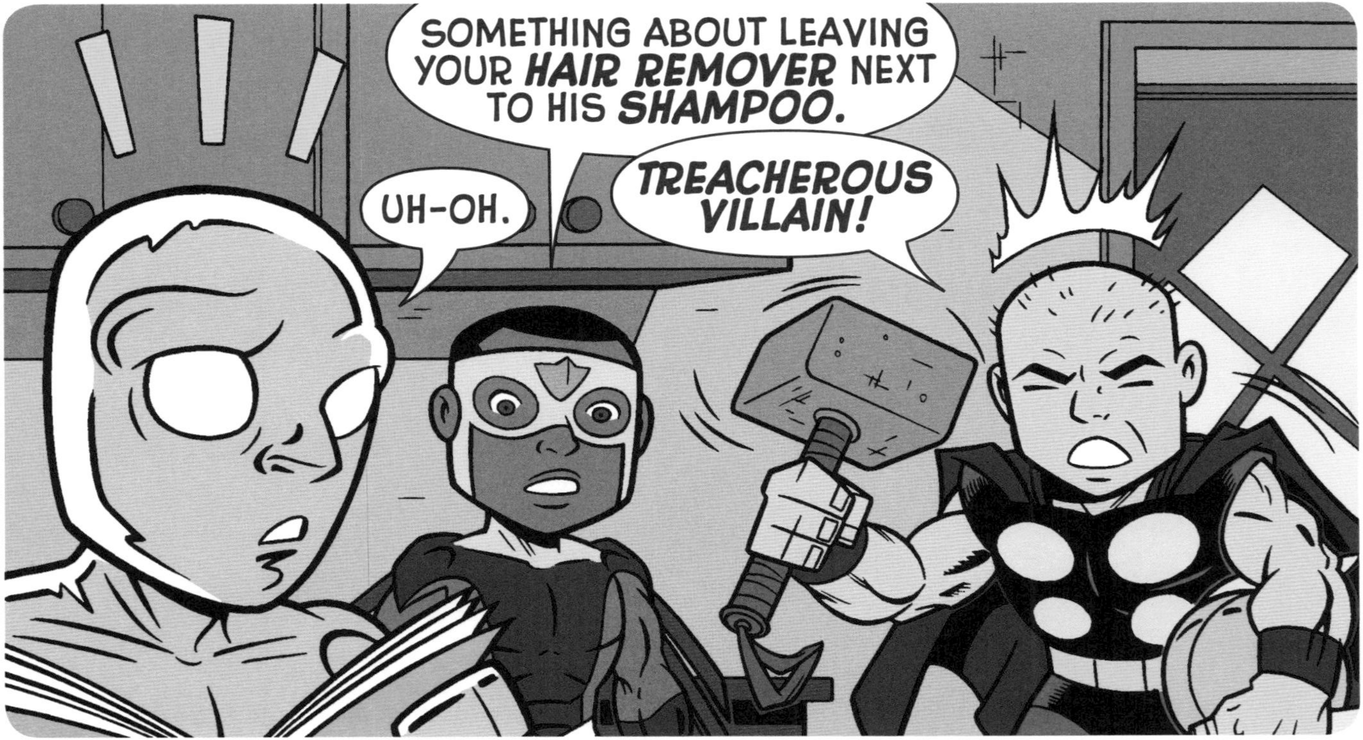
SOMETHING ABOUT LEAVING YOUR HAIR REMOVER NEXT TO HIS SHAMPOO.
UH-OH.
TREACHEROUS VILLAIN!

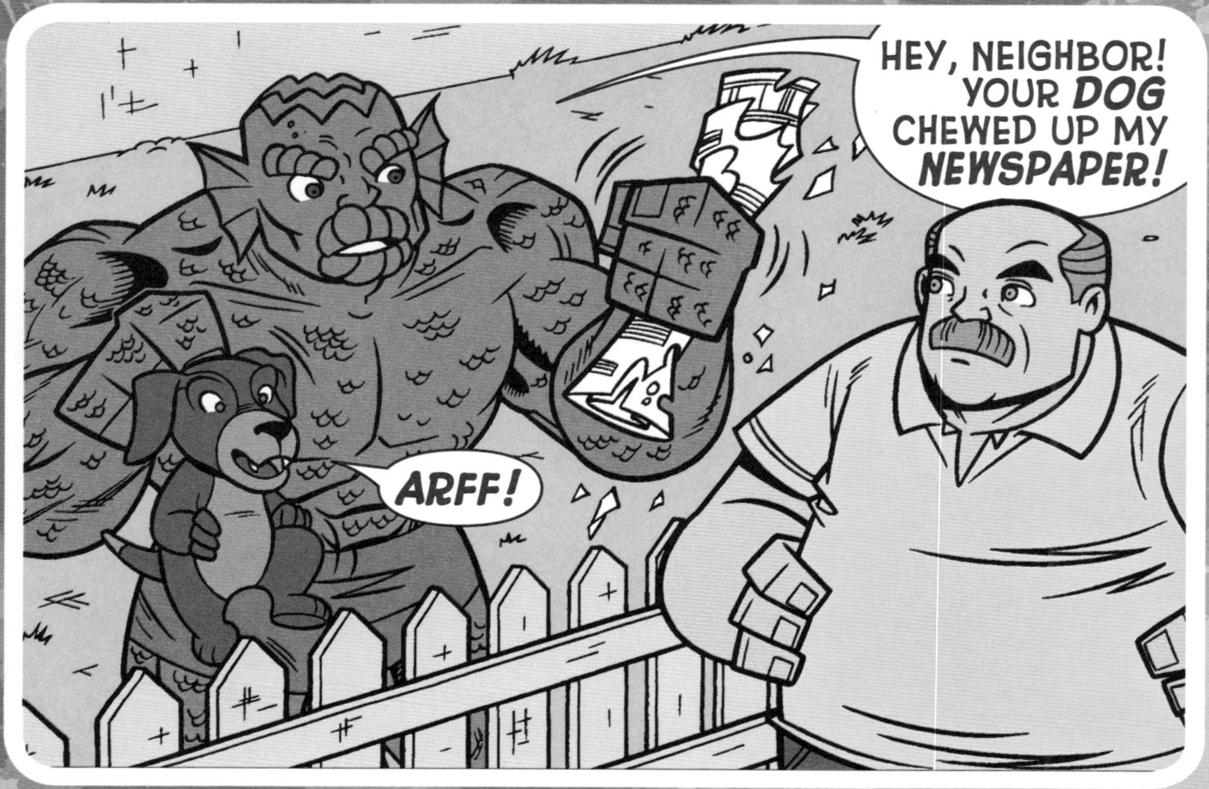
HEY, NEIGHBOR! YOUR DOG CHEWED UP MY NEWSPAPER!
ARFF!

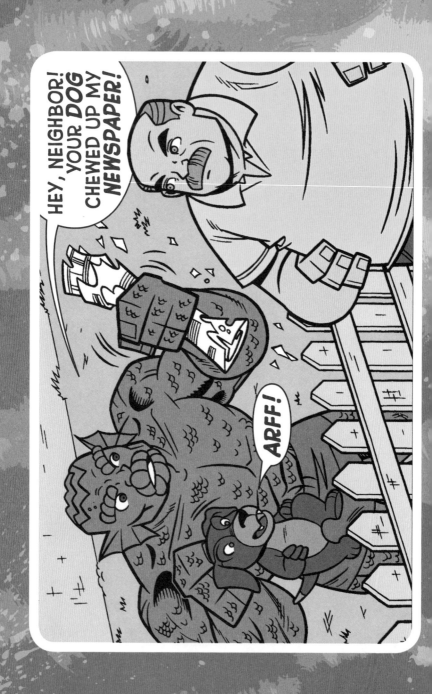

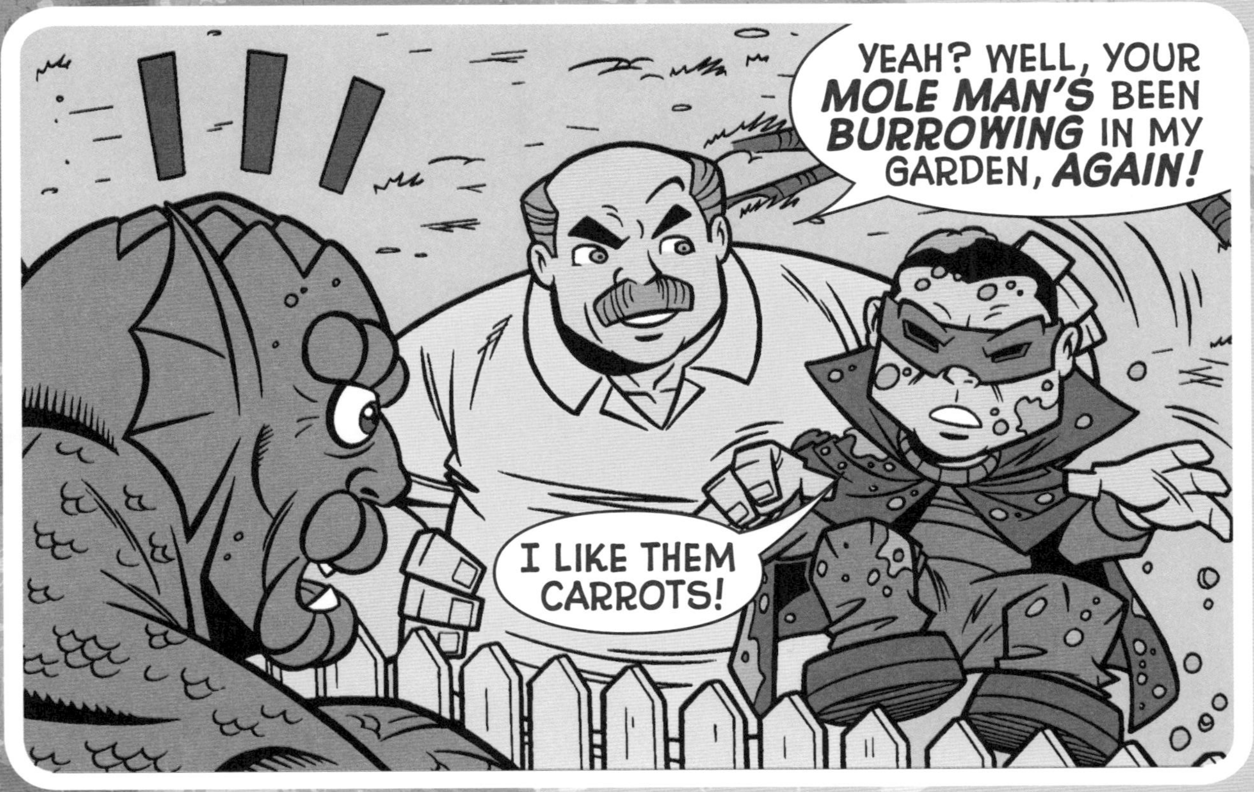
YEAH? WELL, YOUR *MOLE MAN'S* BEEN *BURROWING* IN MY GARDEN, *AGAIN!*
I LIKE THEM CARROTS!

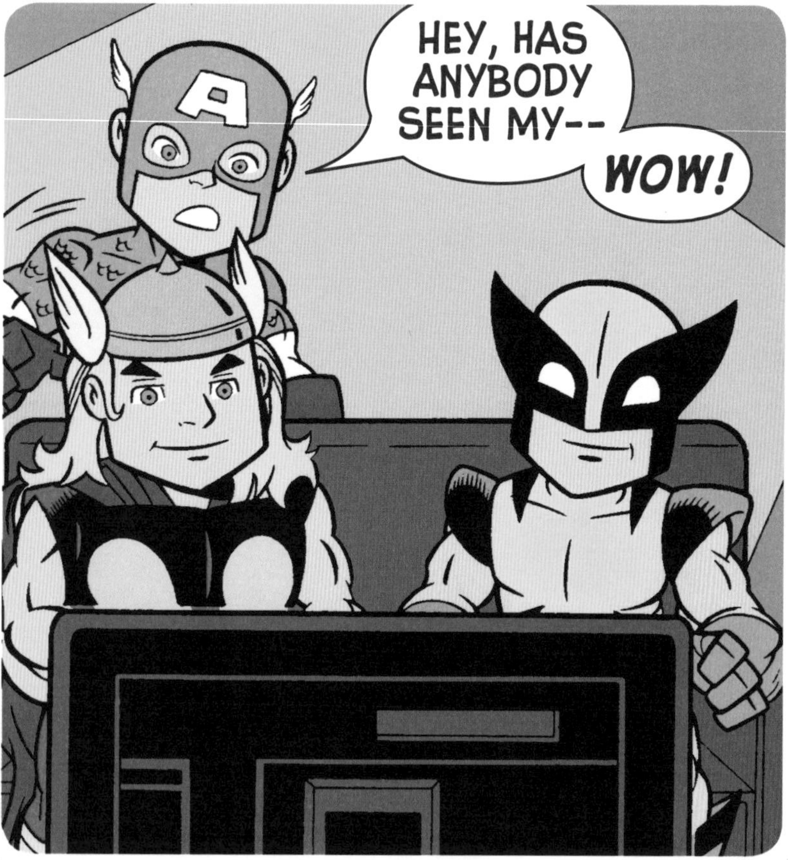
HEY, HAS ANYBODY SEEN MY--
WOW!

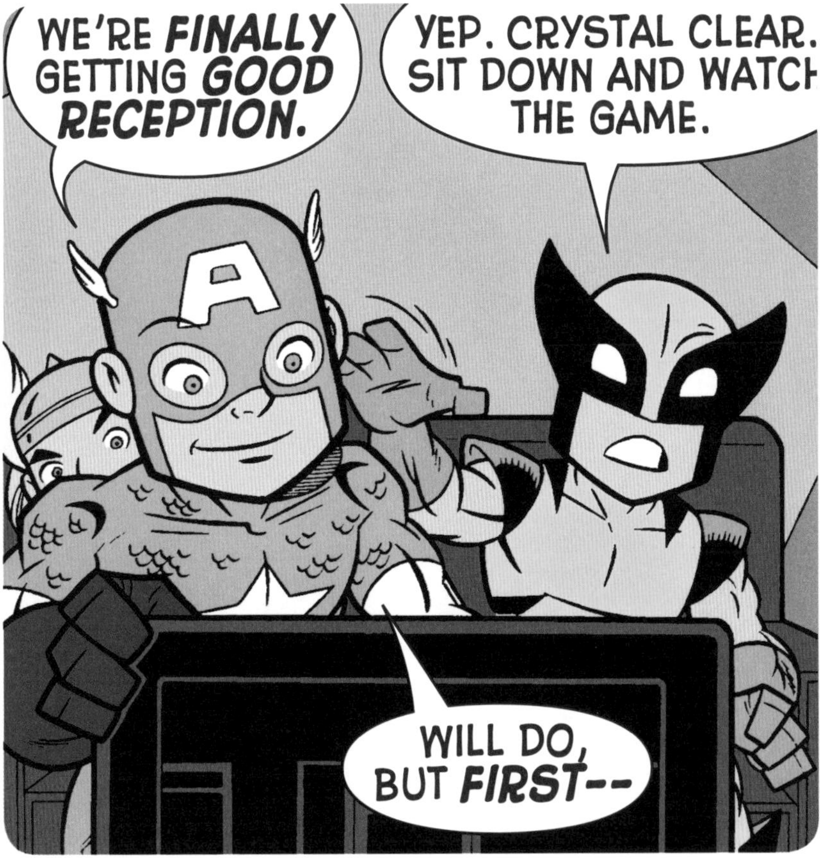
WE'RE FINALLY GETTING GOOD RECEPTION.
YEP. CRYSTAL CLEAR. SIT DOWN AND WATCH THE GAME.
WILL DO, BUT FIRST--

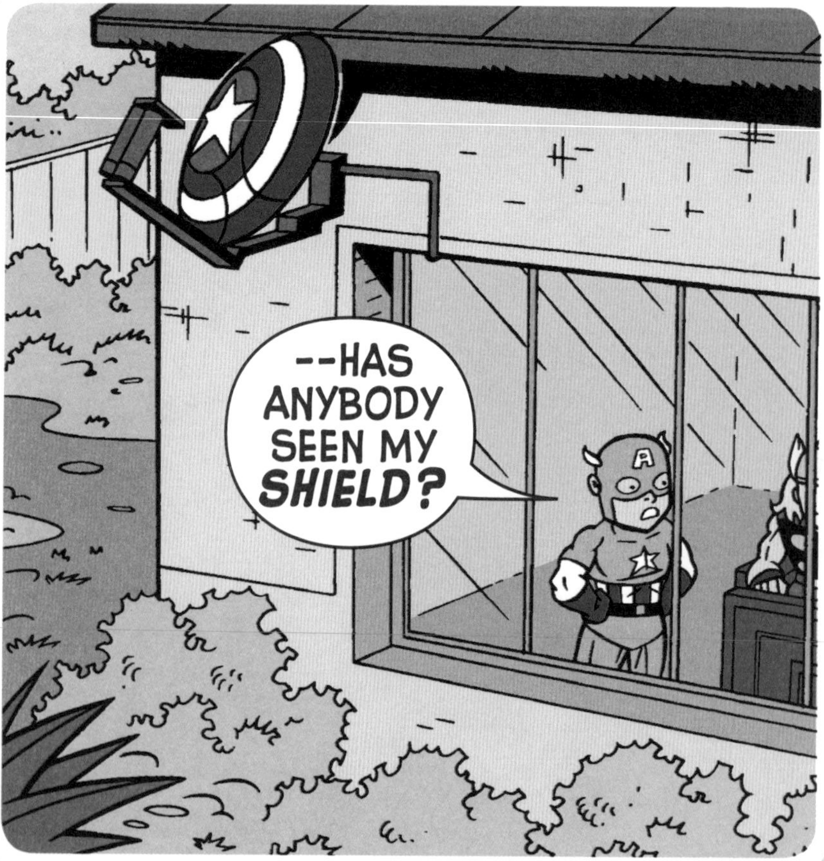
--HAS ANYBODY SEEN MY *SHIELD*?

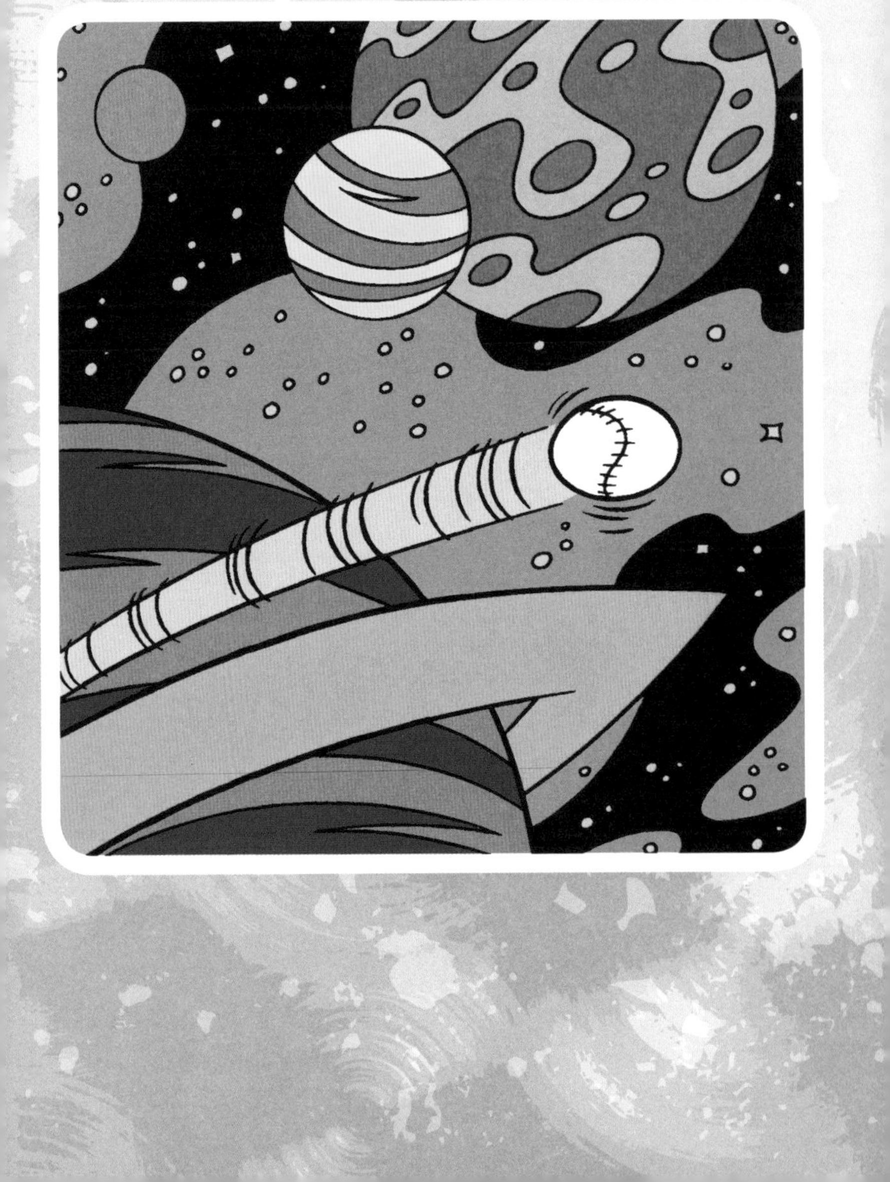

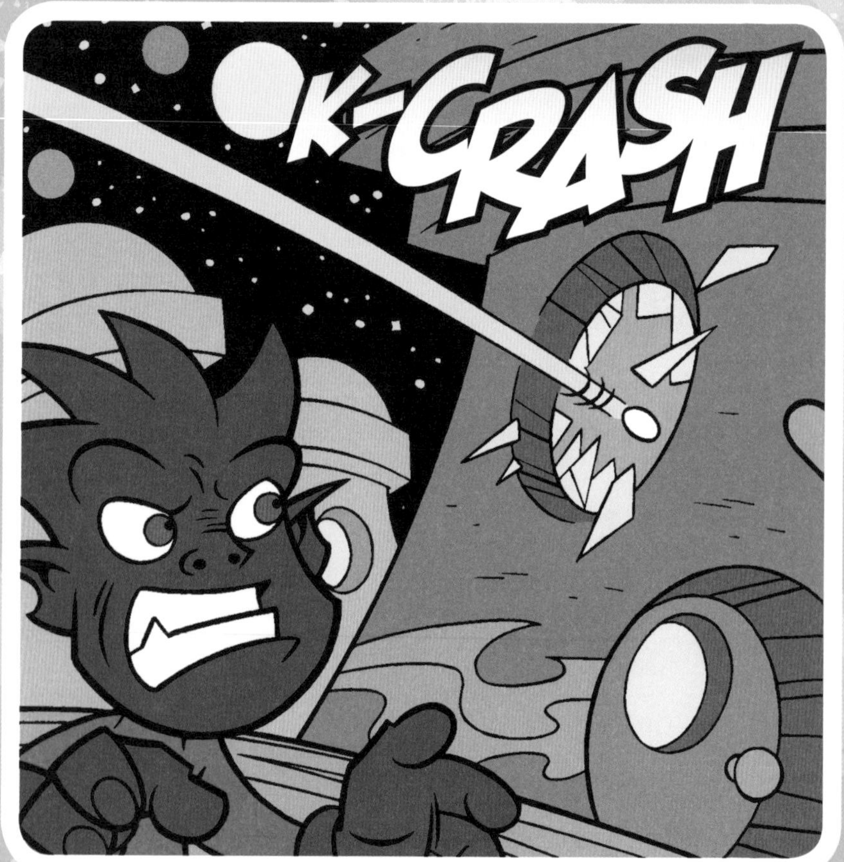
K-CRASH

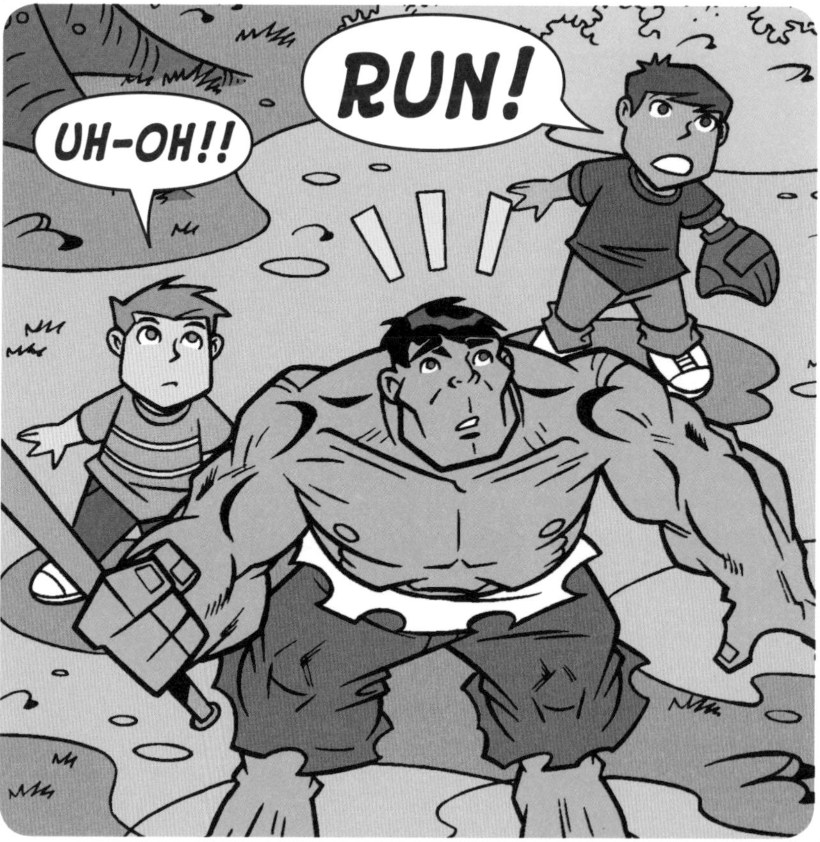
UH-OH!!
RUN!

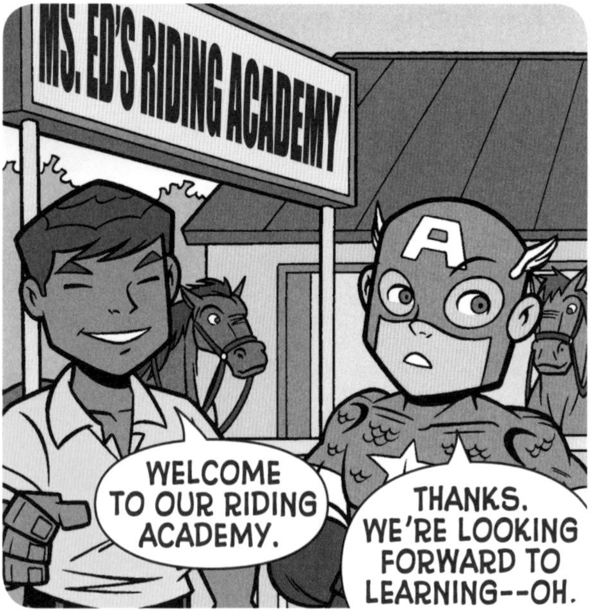
MS. ED'S RIDING ACADEMY
WELCOME TO OUR RIDING ACADEMY.
THANKS. WE'RE LOOKING FORWARD TO LEARNING--OH.

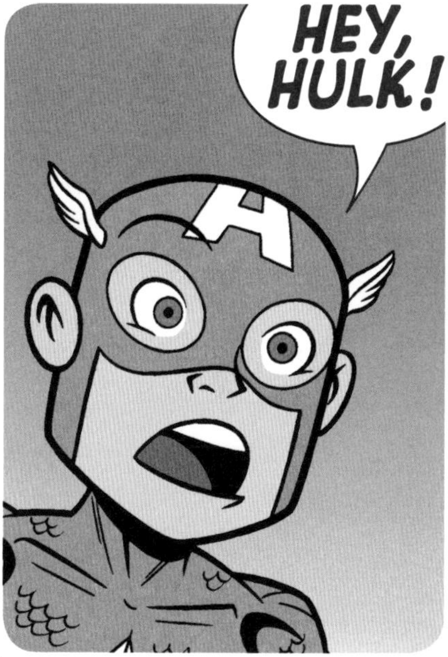
HEY, HULK!

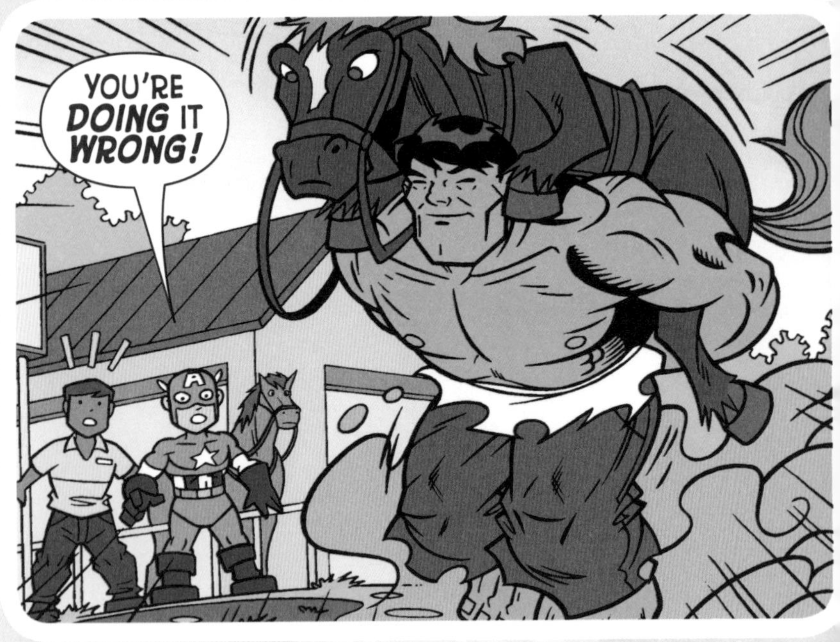
YOU'RE DOING IT WRONG!

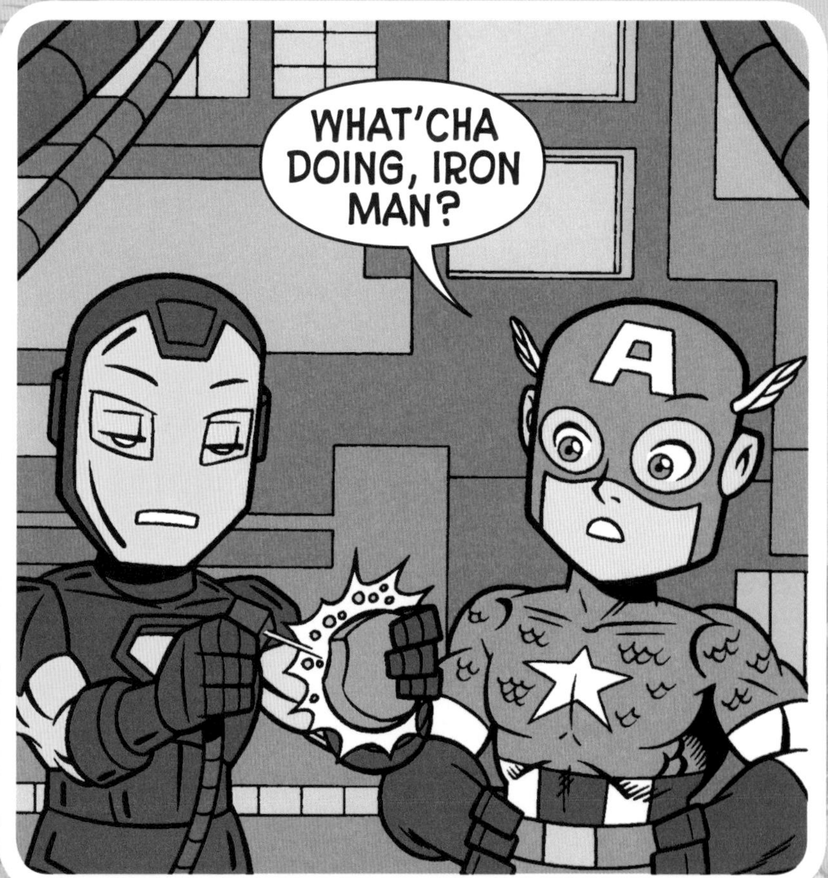
WHAT'CHA DOING, IRON MAN?

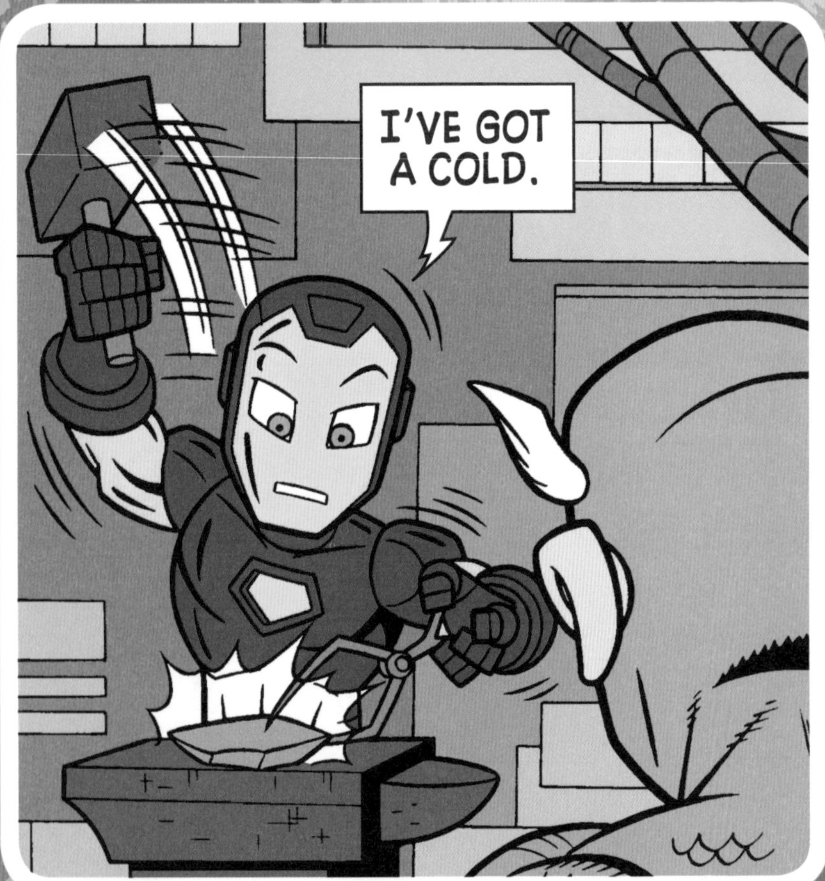
I'VE GOT
A COLD.

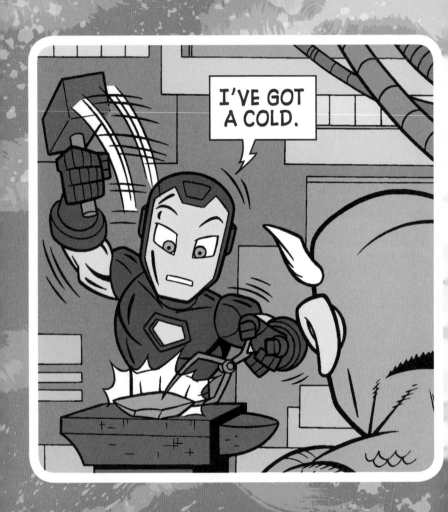

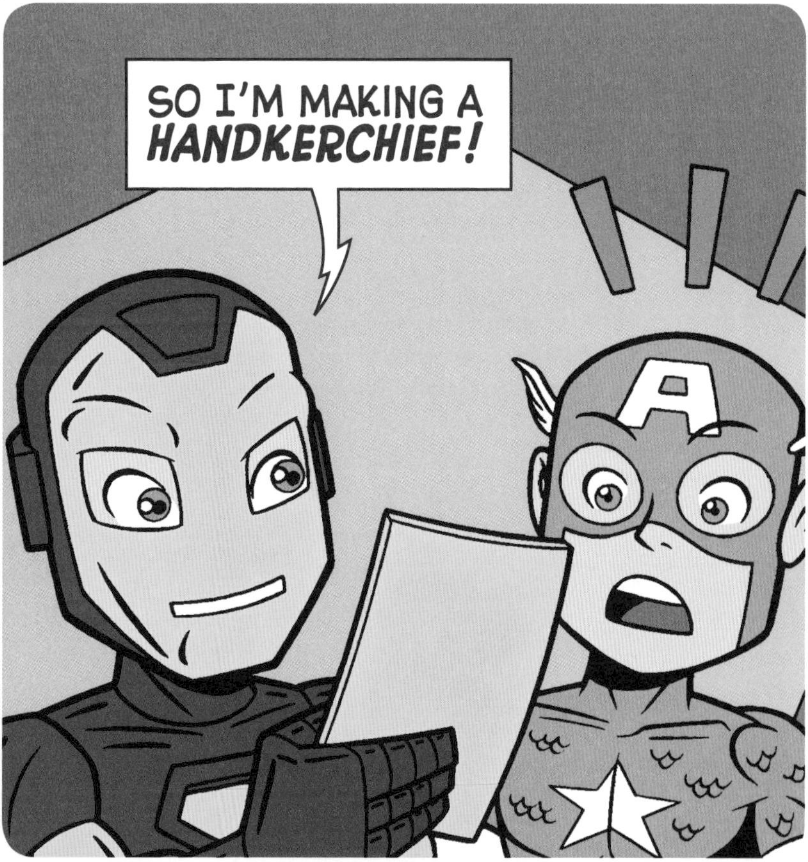
SO I'M MAKING A *HANDKERCHIEF!*

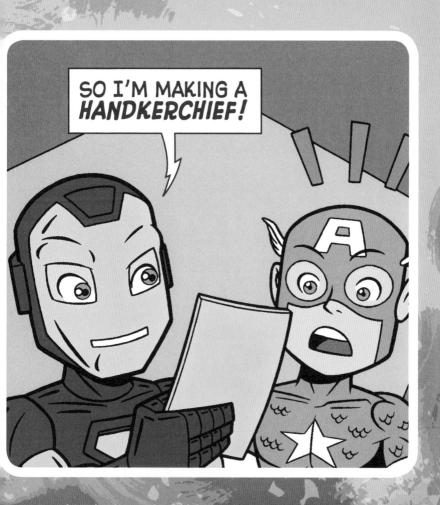

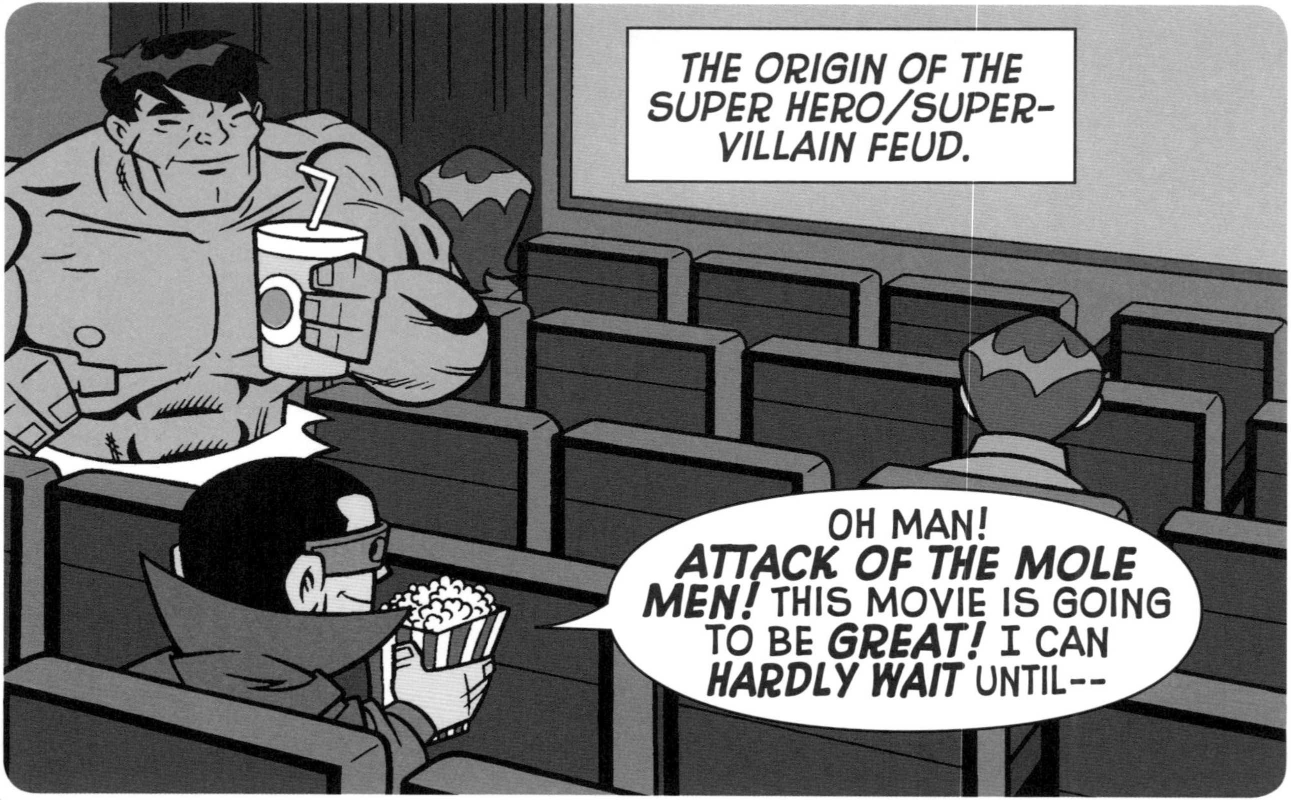
THE ORIGIN OF THE SUPER HERO/SUPER-VILLAIN FEUD.
OH MAN! ATTACK OF THE MOLE MEN! THIS MOVIE IS GOING TO BE GREAT! I CAN HARDLY WAIT UNTIL--

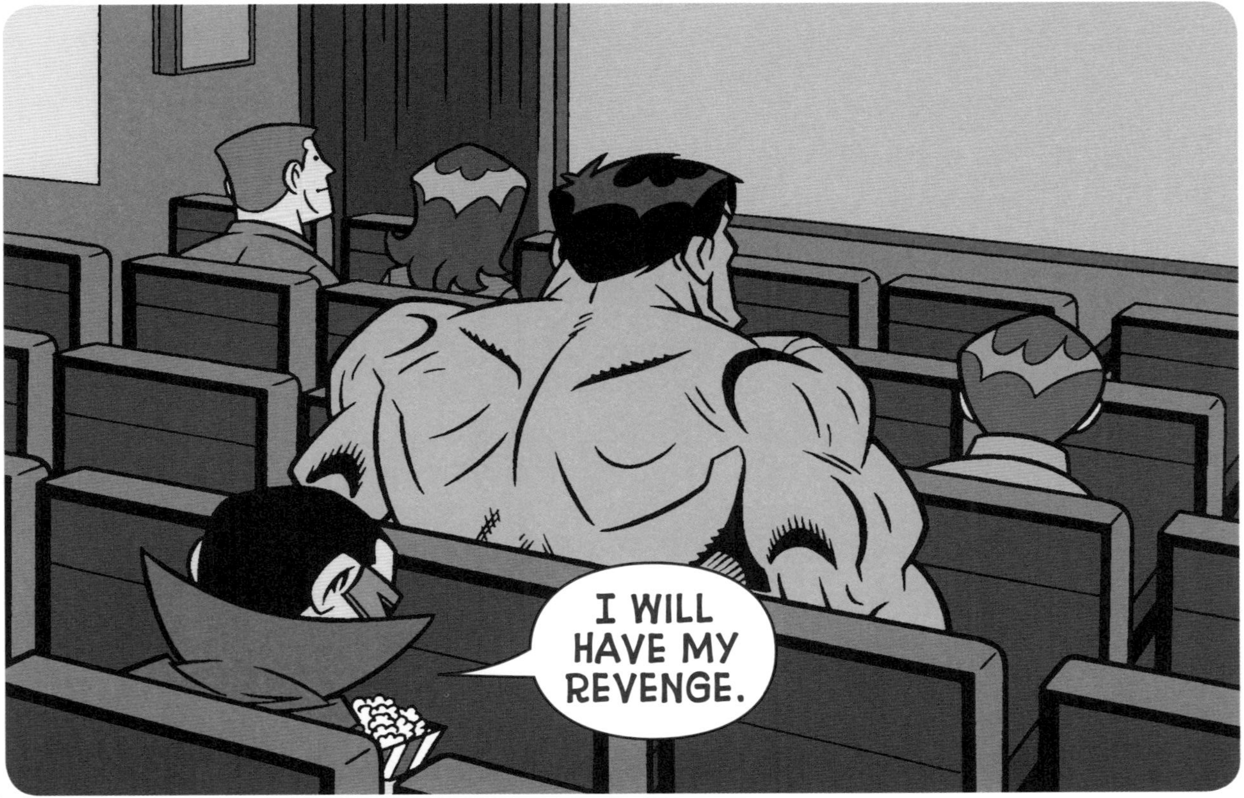
I WILL HAVE MY REVENGE.

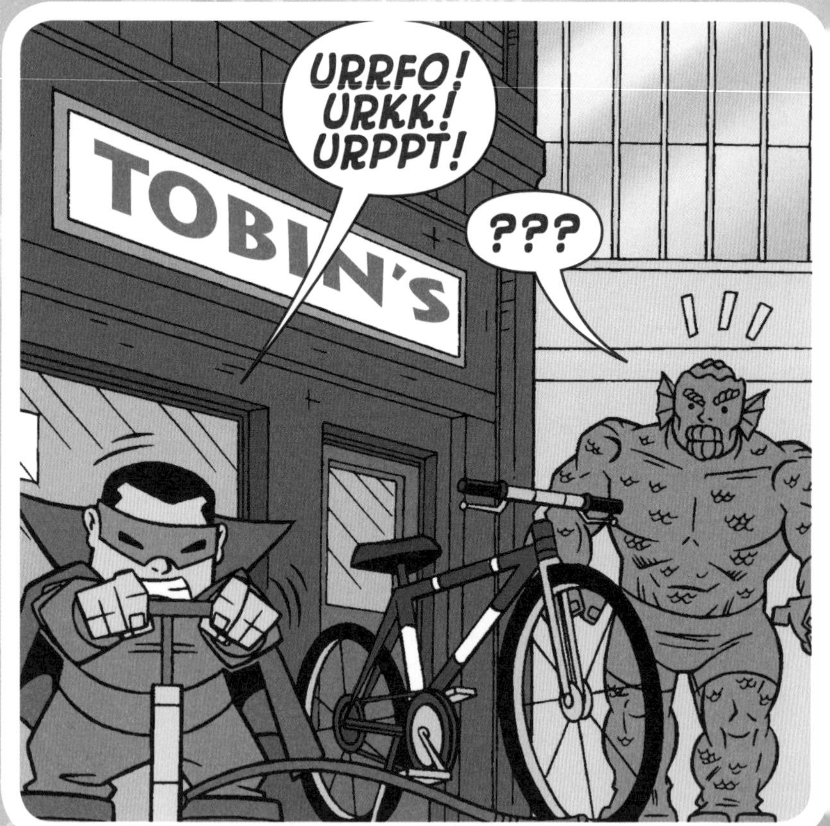
URRFO! URKK! URPPT!
???
TOBIN'S

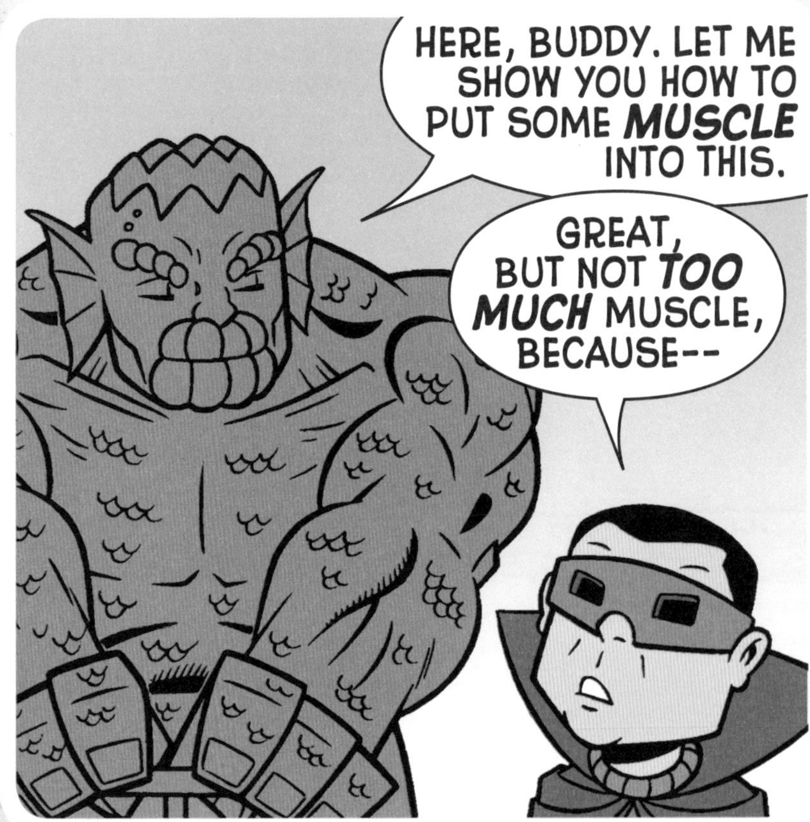
HERE, BUDDY. LET ME SHOW YOU HOW TO PUT SOME *MUSCLE* INTO THIS.
GREAT, BUT NOT *TOO MUCH* MUSCLE, BECAUSE--

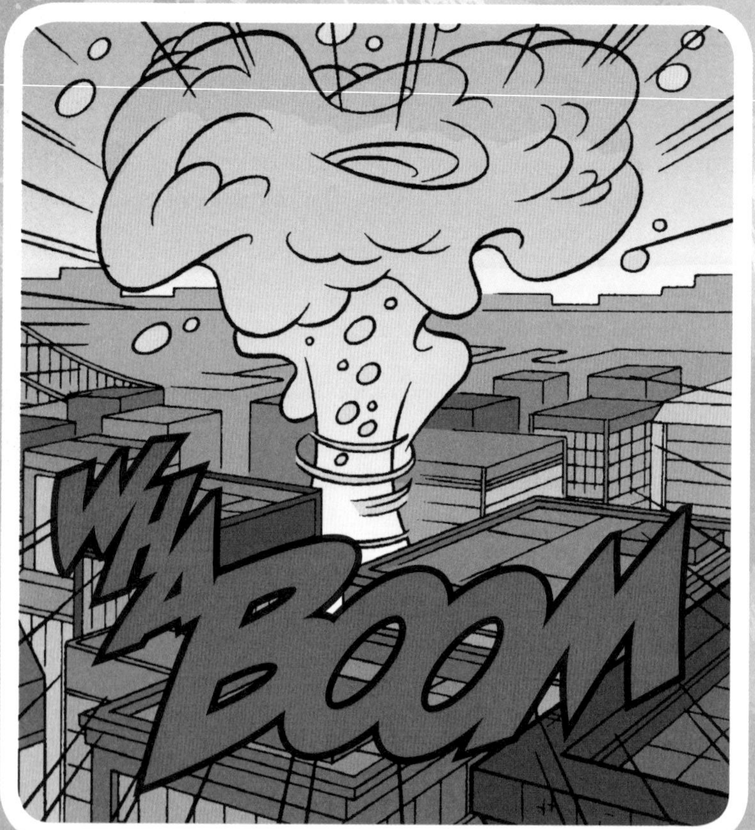
WHA-BOOM

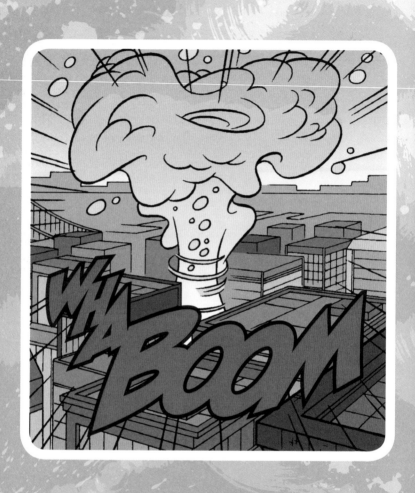

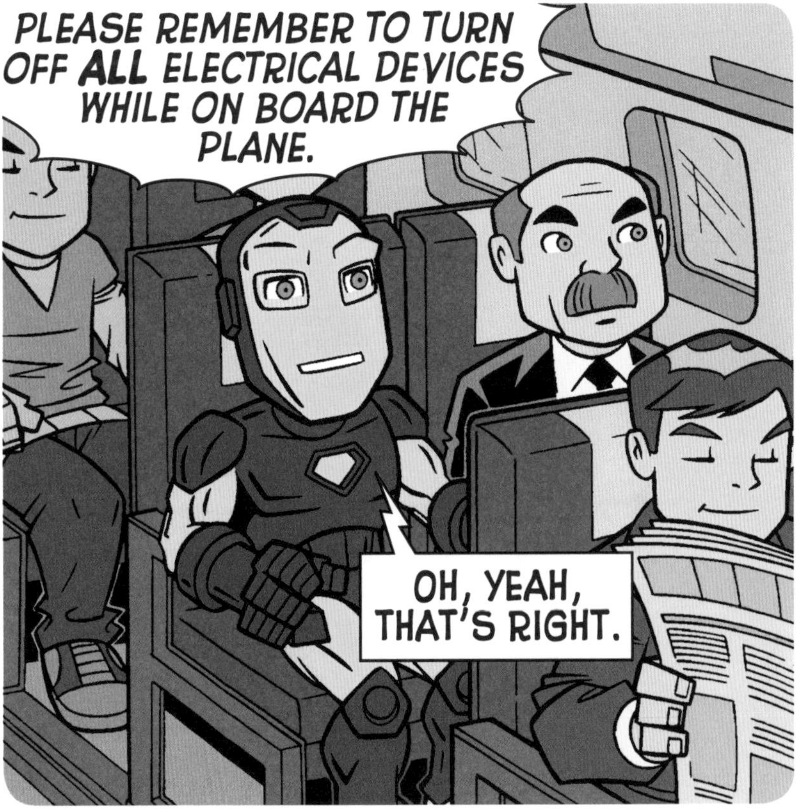
PLEASE REMEMBER TO TURN OFF ALL ELECTRICAL DEVICES WHILE ON BOARD THE PLANE.
OH, YEAH, THAT'S RIGHT.

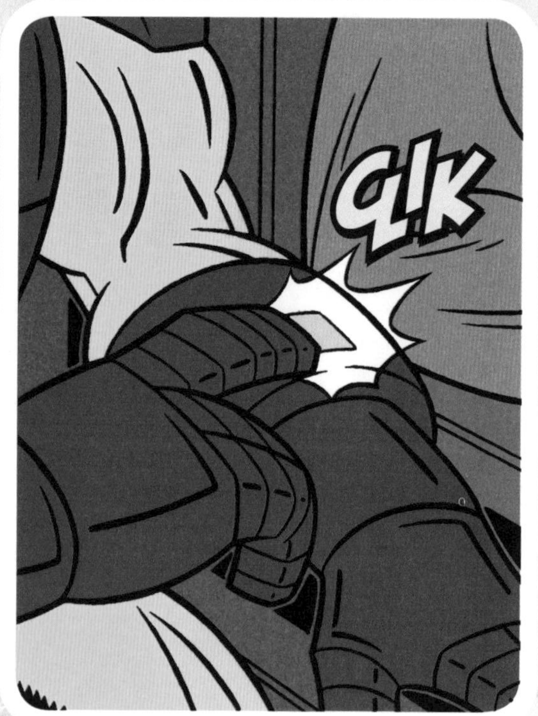
GLK

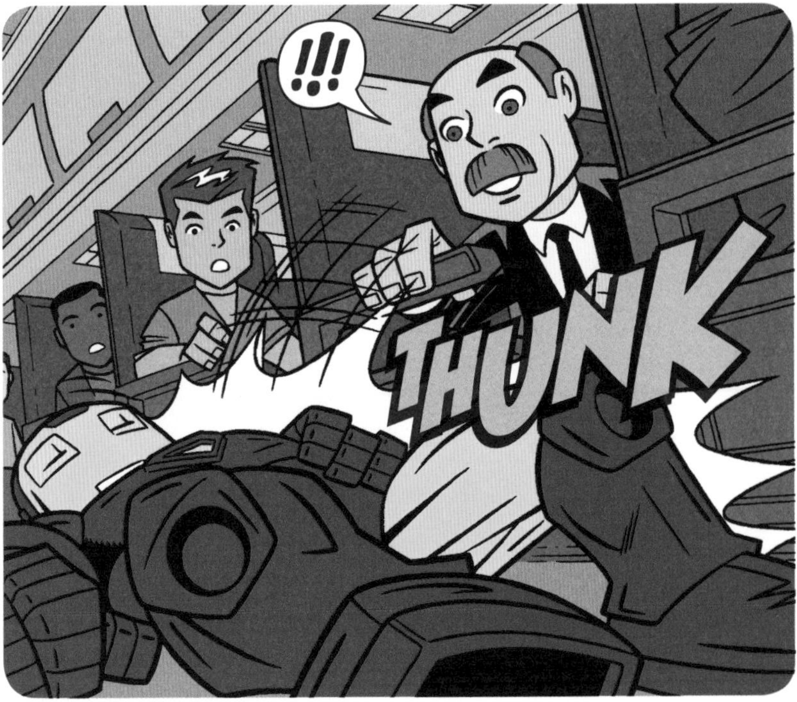

!!!
THUNK

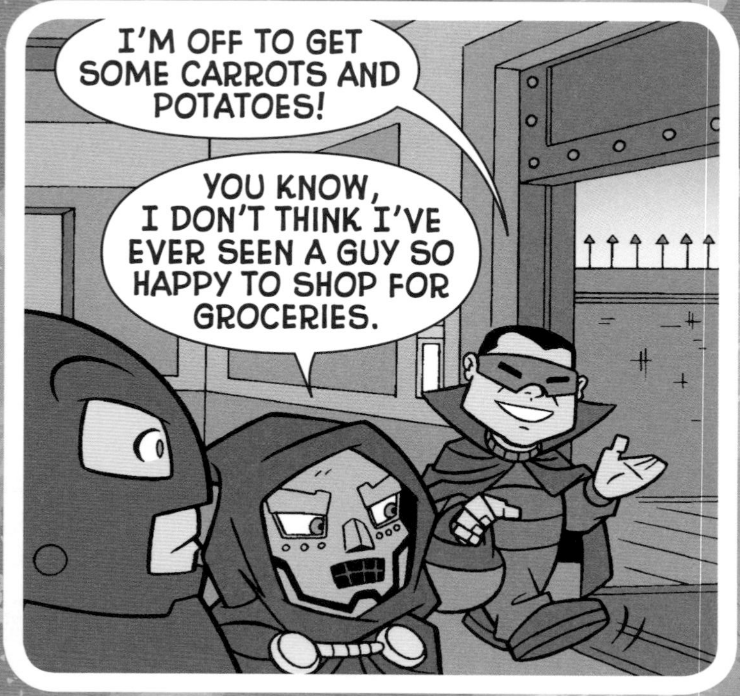
I'M OFF TO GET SOME CARROTS AND POTATOES!
YOU KNOW, I DON'T THINK I'VE EVER SEEN A GUY SO HAPPY TO SHOP FOR GROCERIES.

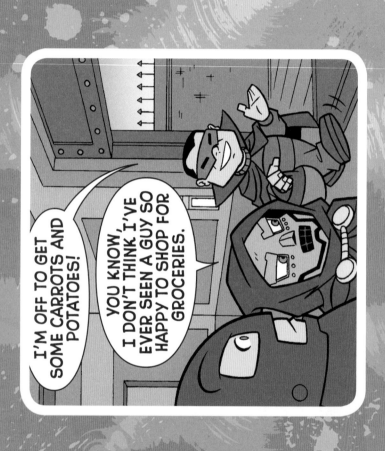

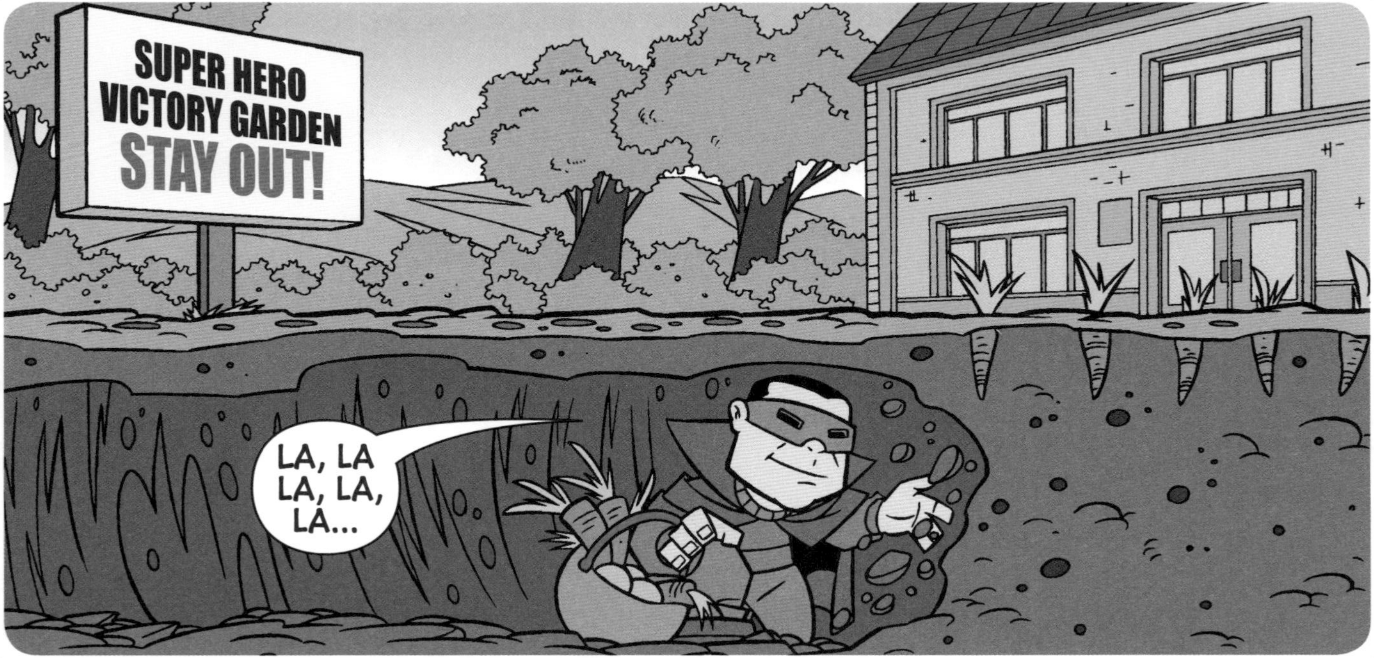
SUPER HERO
VICTORY GARDEN
STAY OUT!
LA, LA LA, LA, LA...

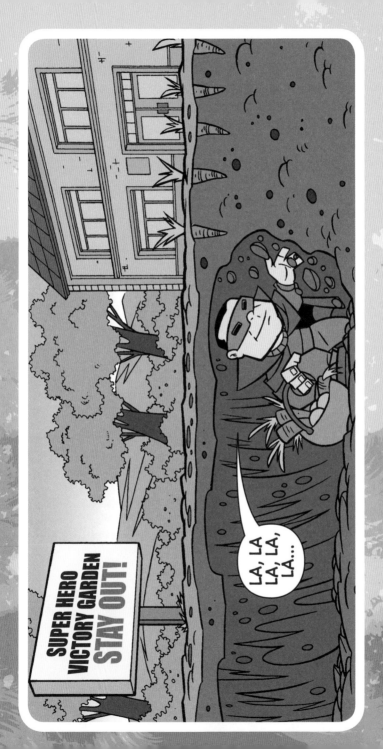

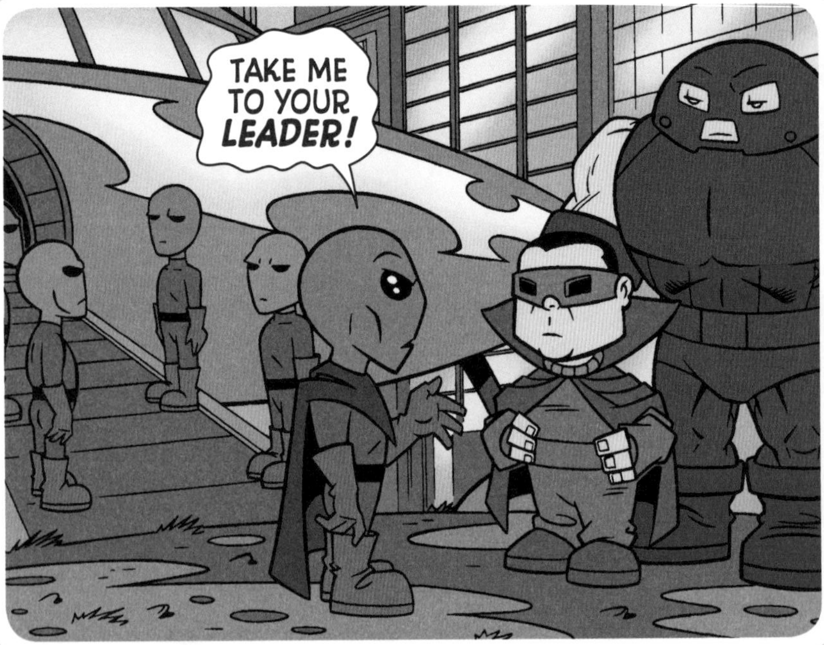
TAKE ME TO YOUR LEADER!

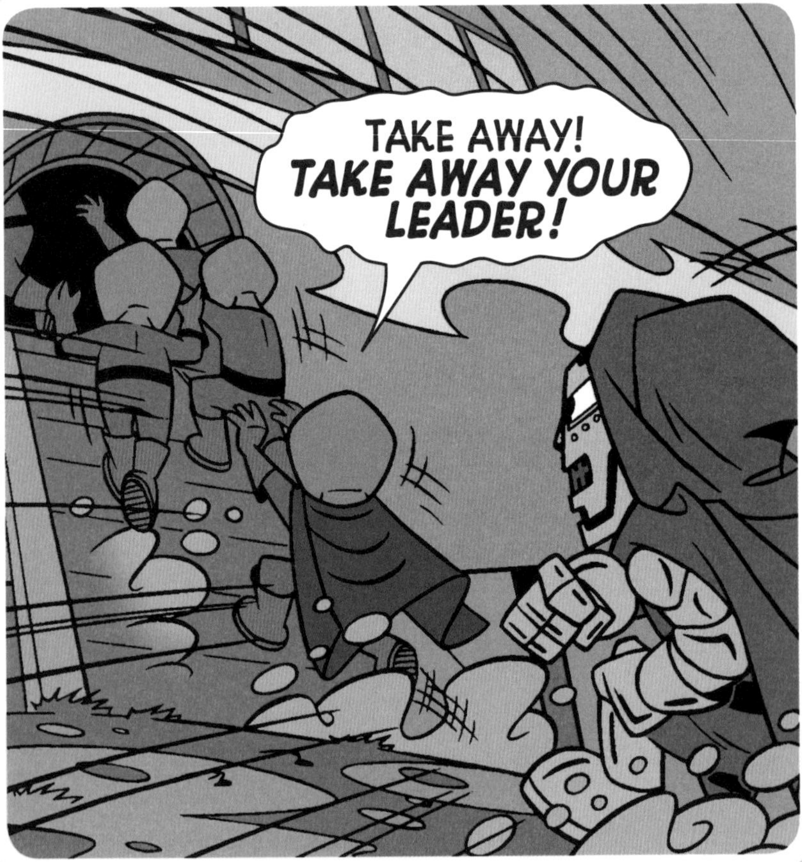
TAKE AWAY!
TAKE AWAY YOUR LEADER!

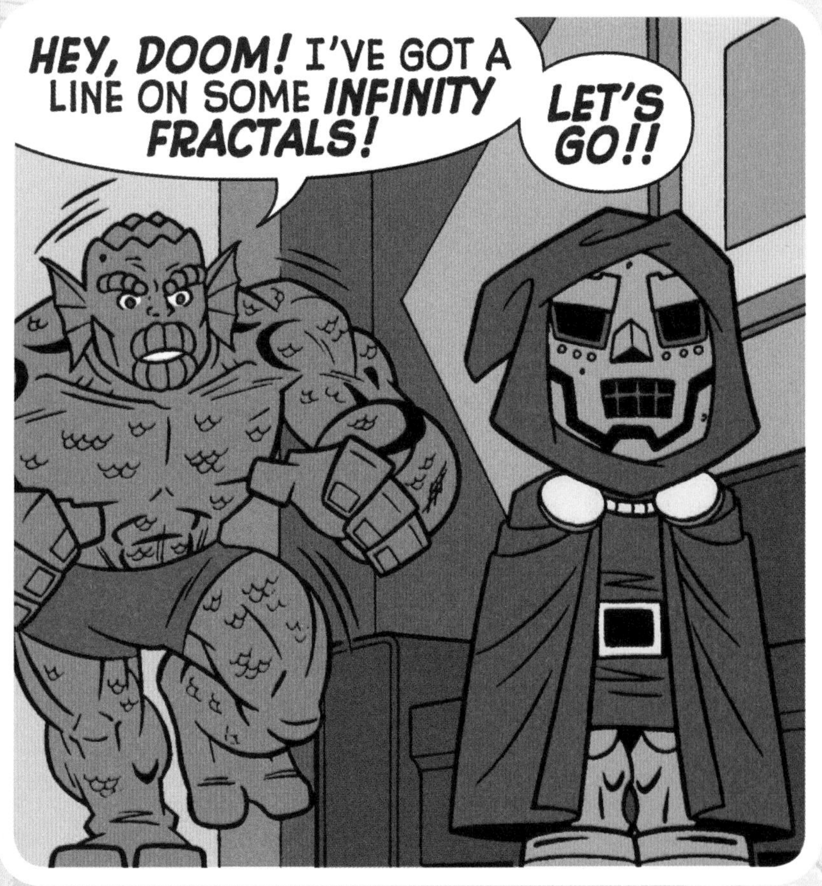
HEY, DOOM! I'VE GOT A LINE ON SOME INFINITY FRACTALS!
LET'S GO!!

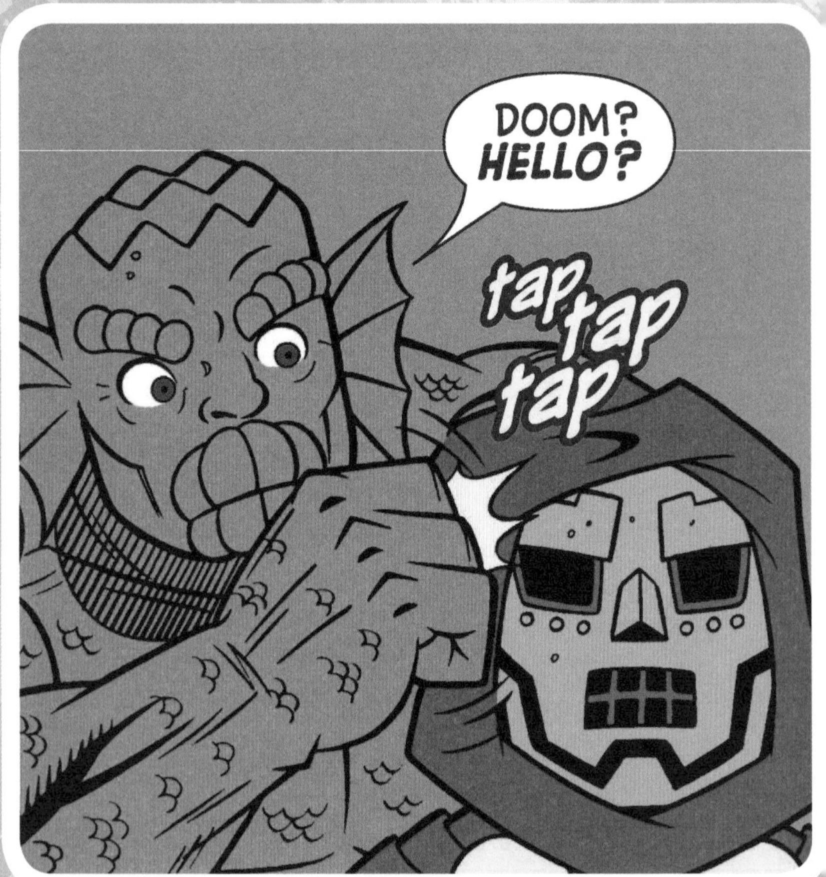
DOOM? HELLO?
tap tap tap

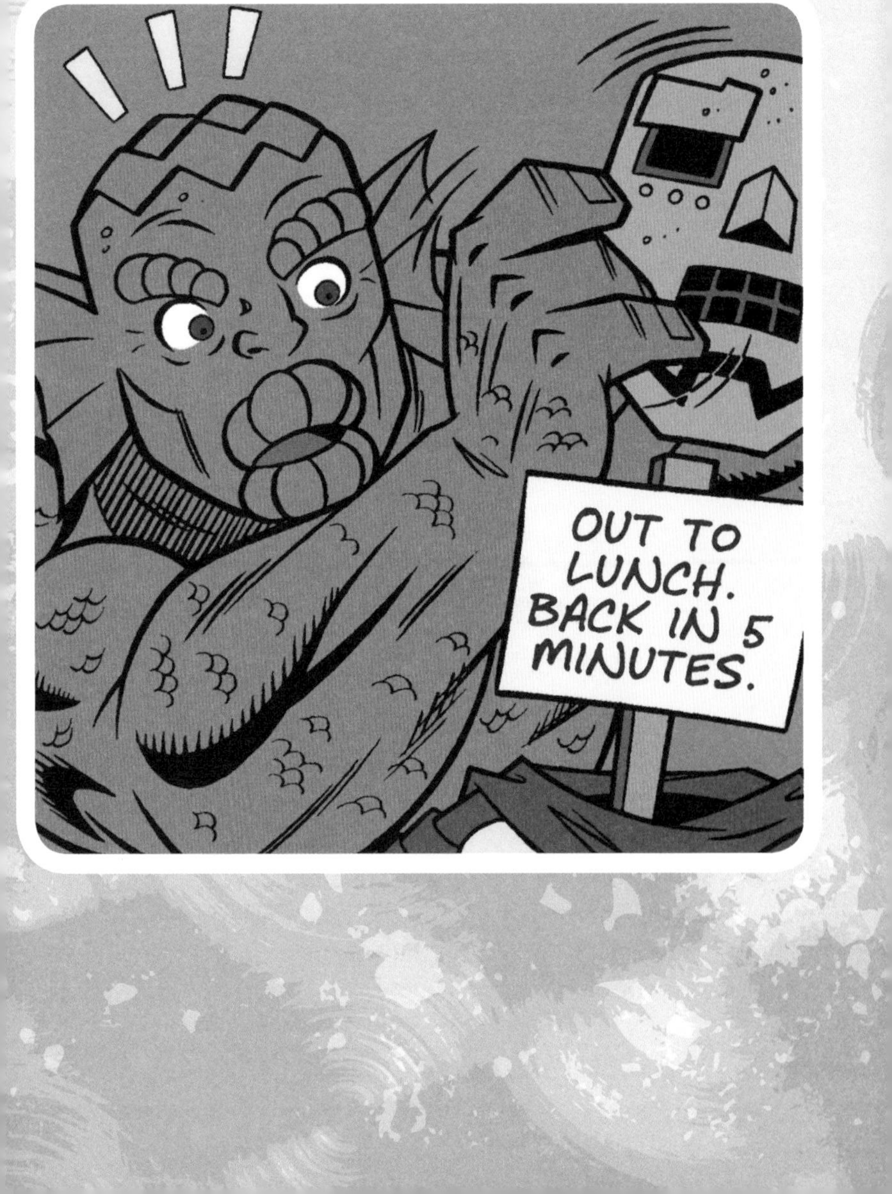
OUT TO LUNCH. BACK IN 5 MINUTES.

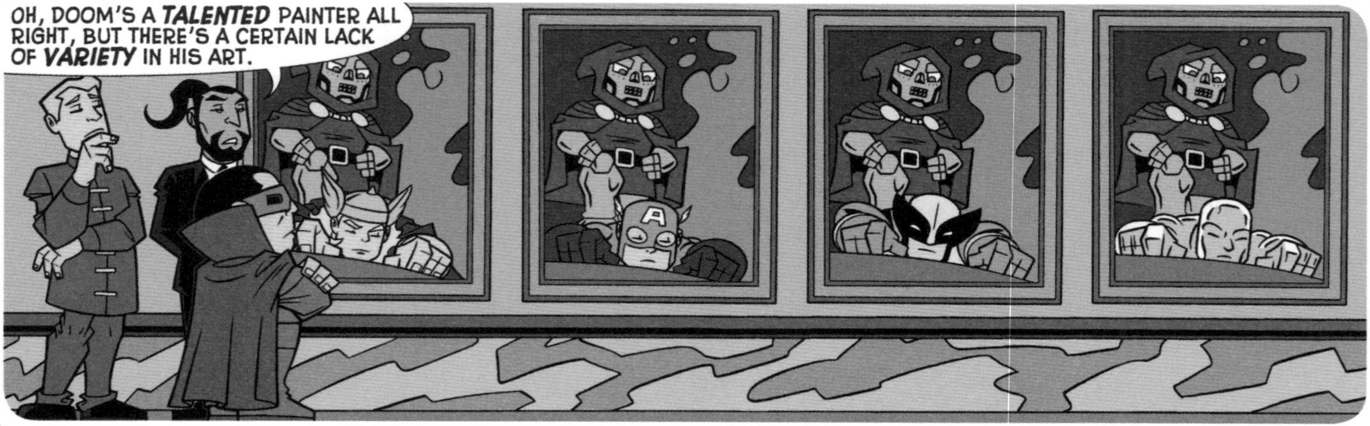
OH, DOOM'S A ***TALENTED*** PAINTER ALL RIGHT, BUT THERE'S A CERTAIN LACK OF ***VARIETY*** IN HIS ART.

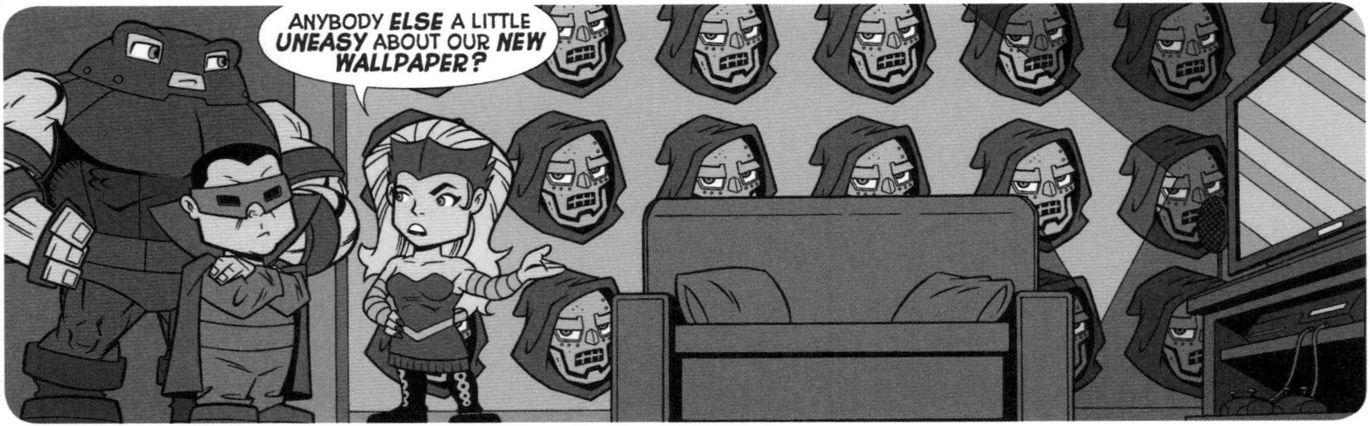
ANYBODY ELSE A LITTLE UNEASY ABOUT OUR NEW WALLPAPER?

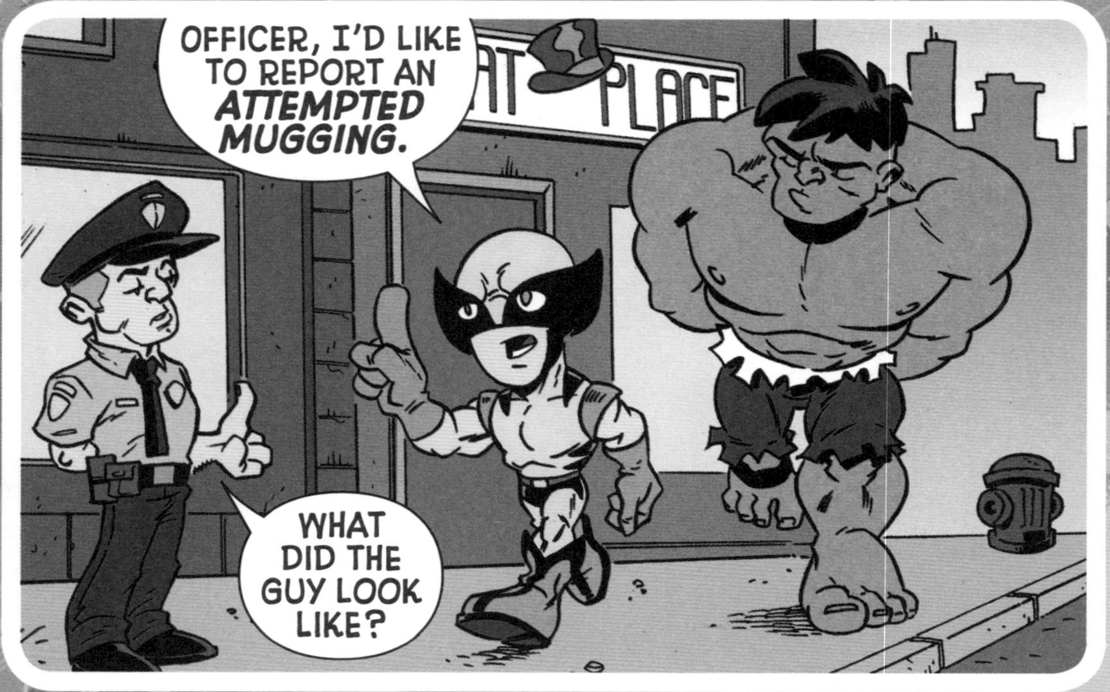
OFFICER, I'D LIKE TO REPORT AN *ATTEMPTED MUGGING.*
WHAT DID THE GUY LOOK LIKE?

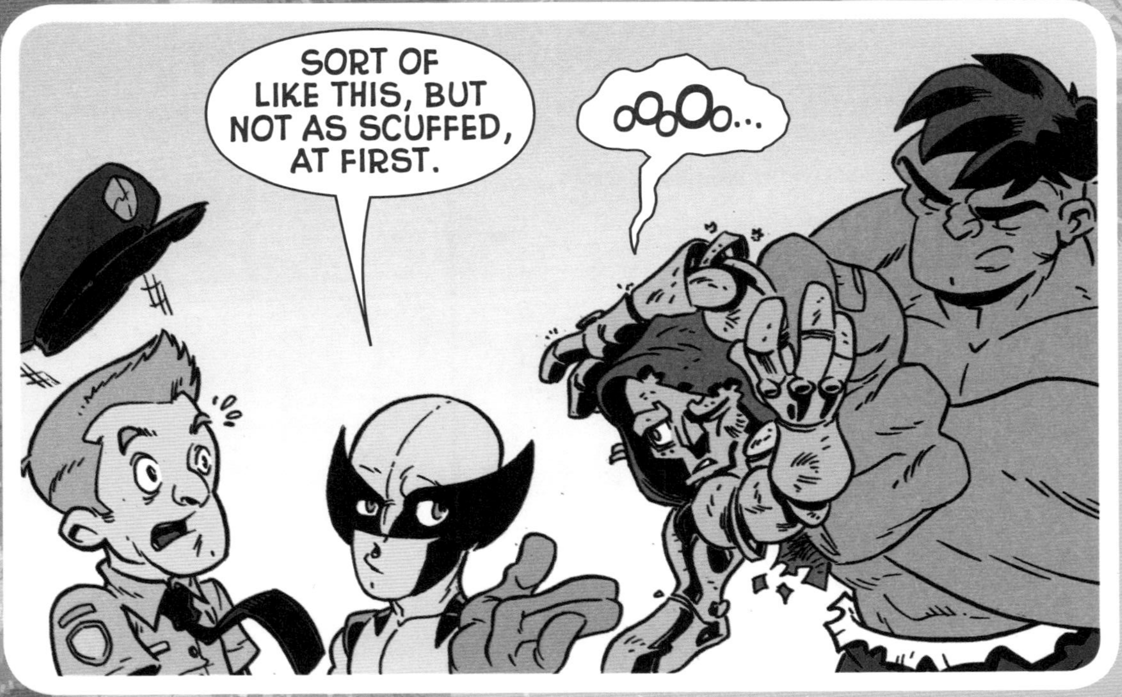
SORT OF LIKE THIS, BUT NOT AS SCUFFED, AT FIRST.
oooOo...

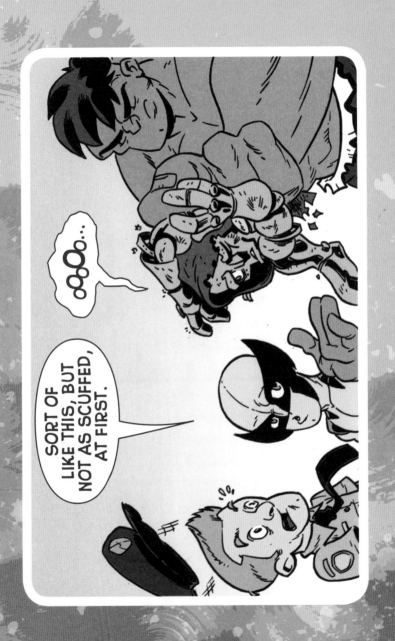

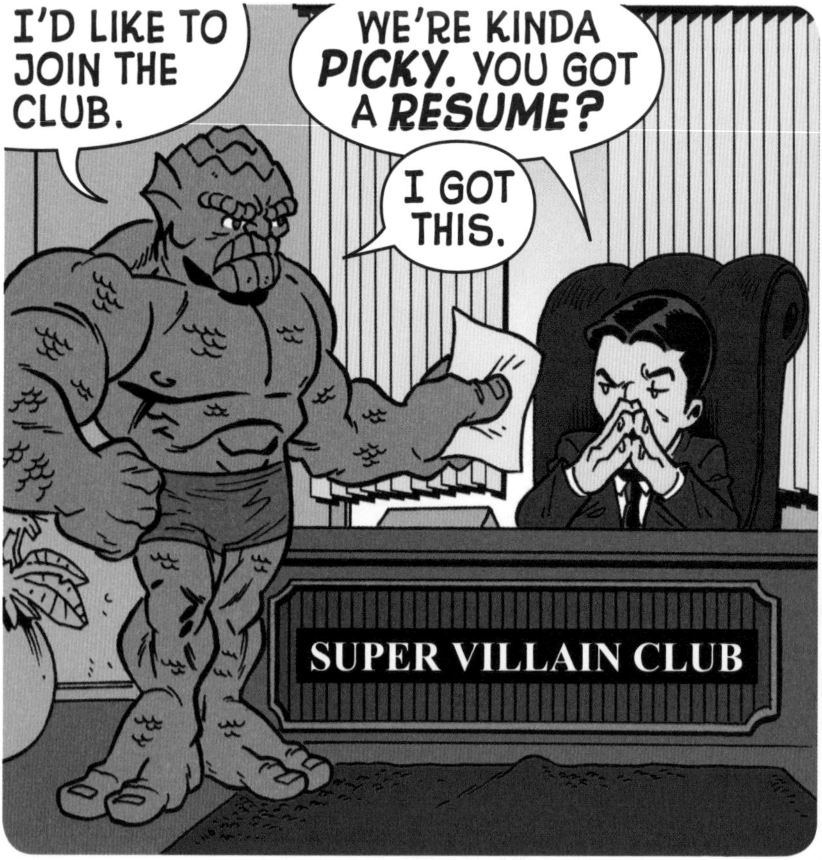
I'D LIKE TO JOIN THE CLUB.
WE'RE KINDA PICKY. YOU GOT A RESUME?
I GOT THIS.
SUPER VILLAIN CLUB

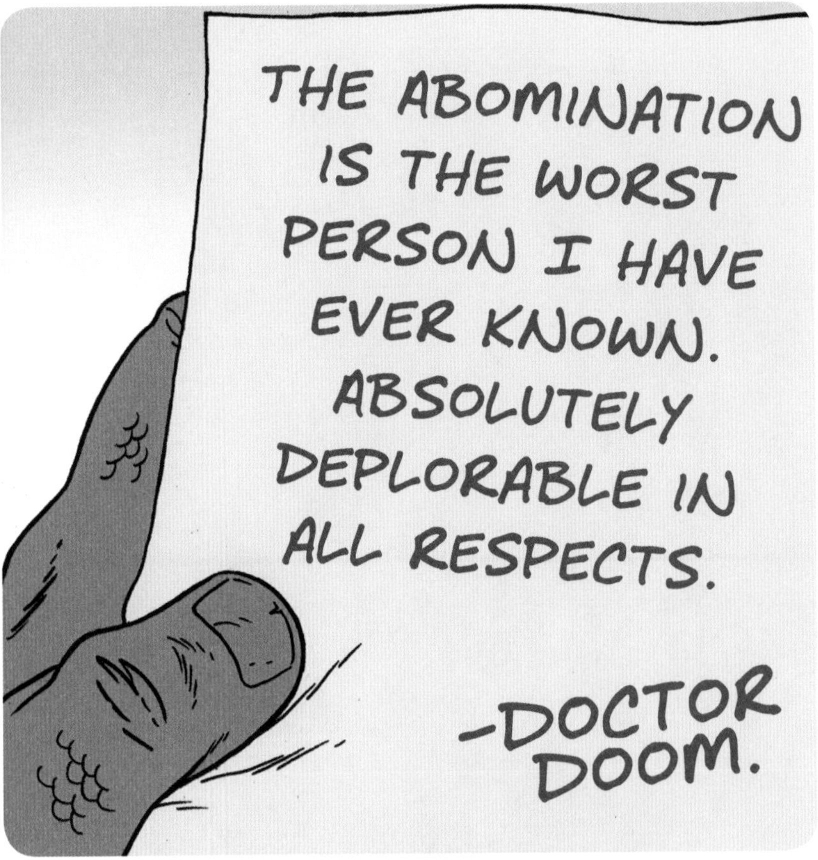
THE ABOMINATION IS THE WORST PERSON I HAVE EVER KNOWN. ABSOLUTELY DEPLORABLE IN ALL RESPECTS.
-DOCTOR DOOM.

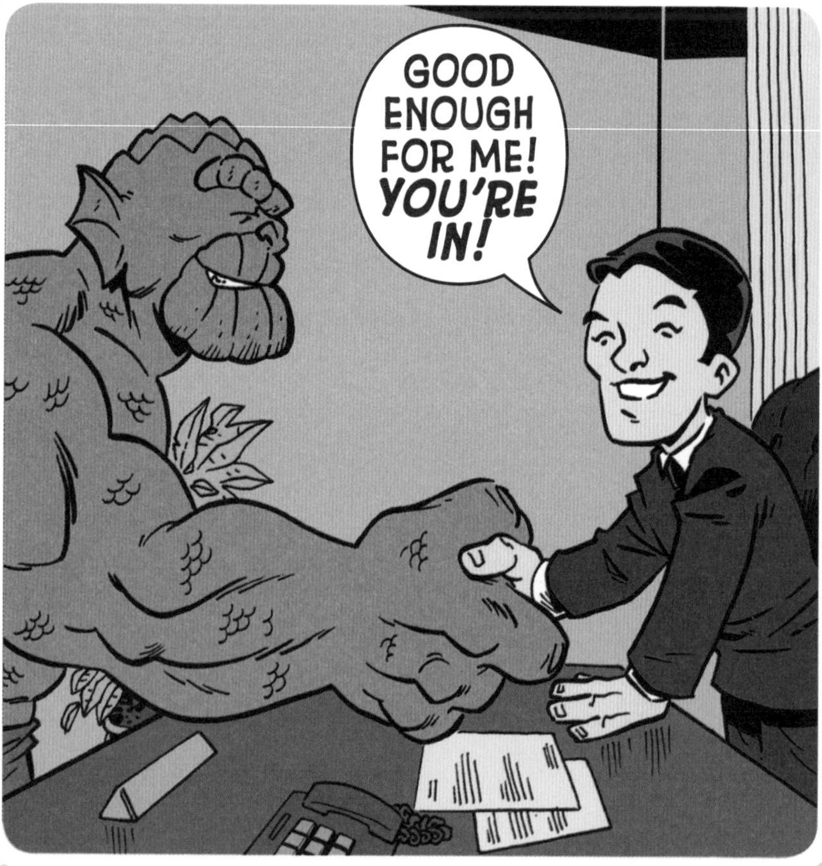
GOOD ENOUGH FOR ME! YOU'RE IN!

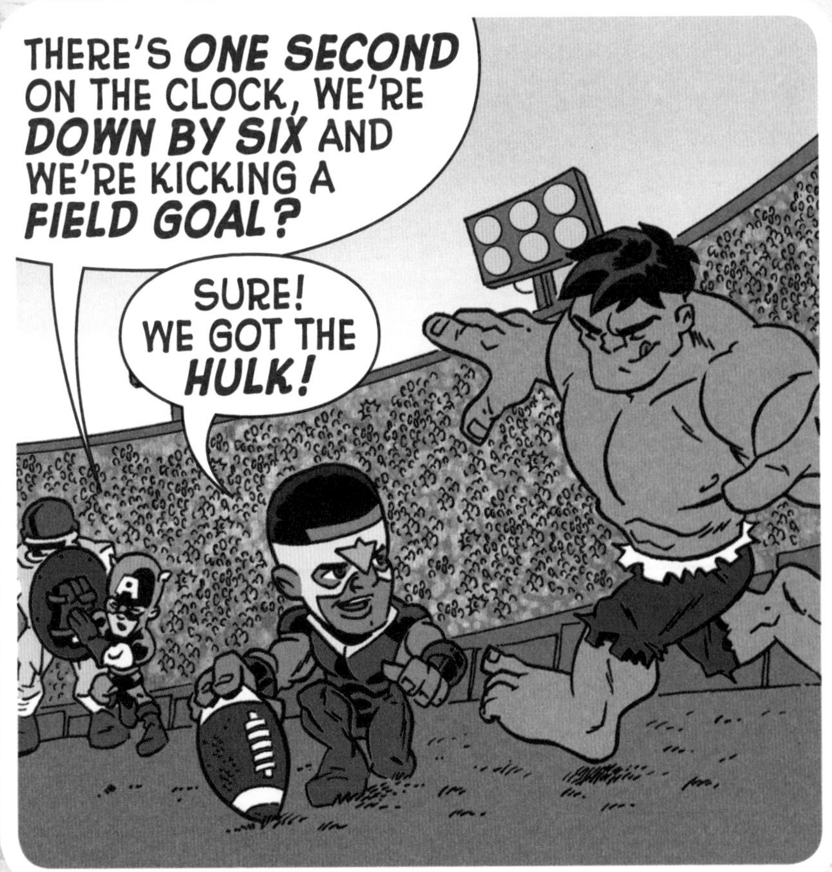
THERE'S ONE SECOND ON THE CLOCK, WE'RE DOWN BY SIX AND WE'RE KICKING A FIELD GOAL?
SURE! WE GOT THE HULK!

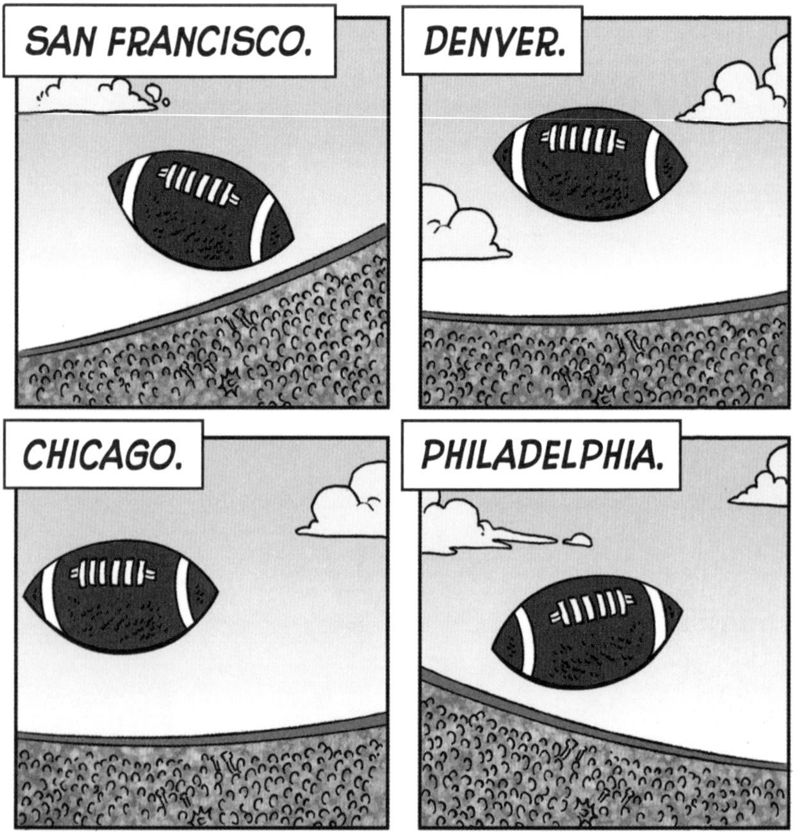
SAN FRANCISCO.
DENVER.
CHICAGO.
PHILADELPHIA.

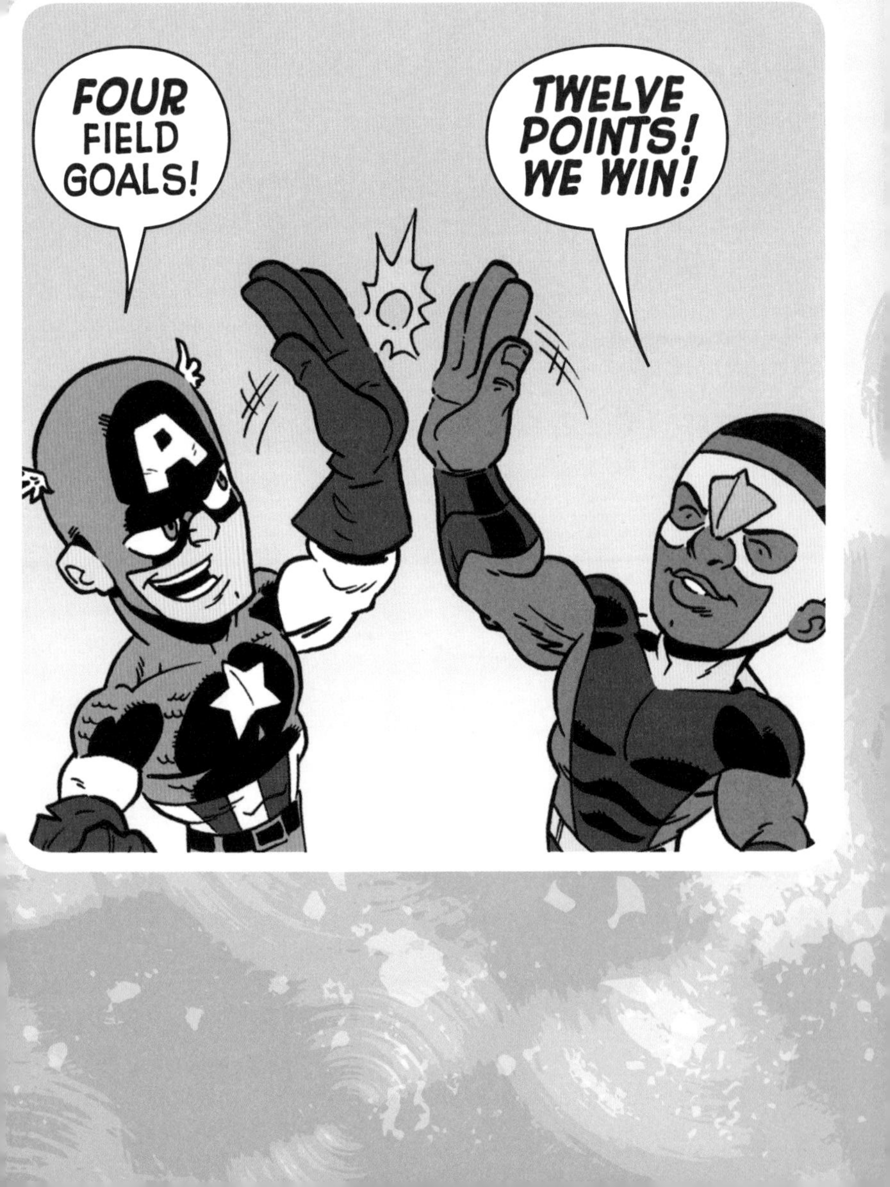
FOUR FIELD GOALS!
TWELVE POINTS! WE WIN!

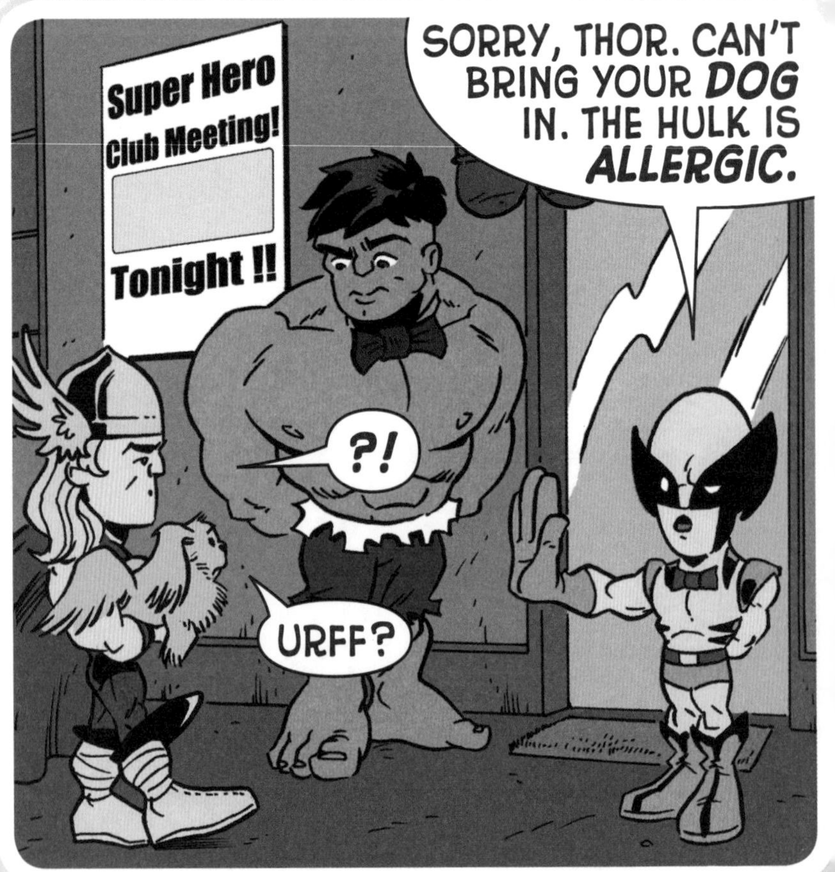

Super Hero
Club Meeting!
Tonight !!
SORRY, THOR. CAN'T BRING YOUR ***DOG*** IN. THE HULK IS ***ALLERGIC.***
?!
URFF?

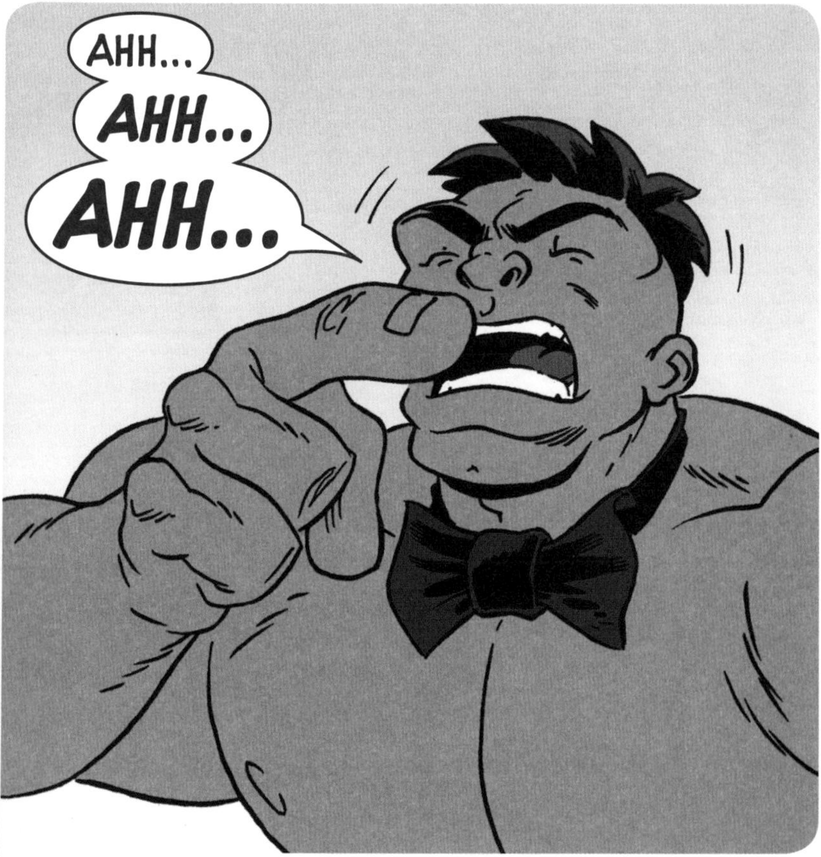
AHH...
AHH...
AHH...

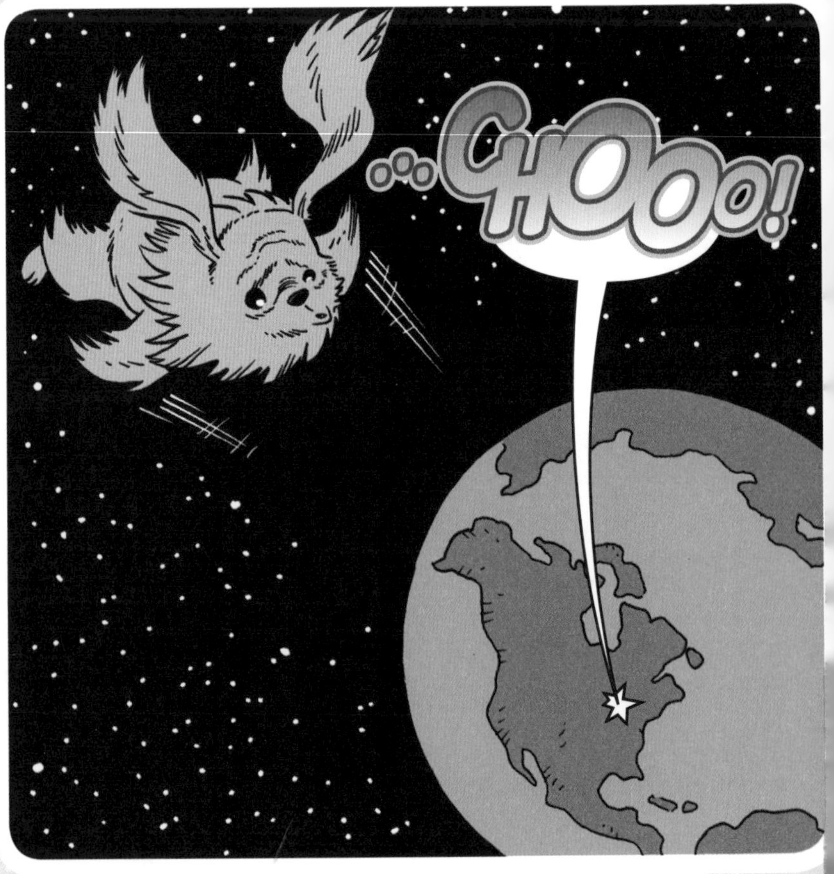
...CHOOOo!